The Game of Forbidden Love

Brad Rudisail

ISBN: 978-0-9883911-3-0

CONTENTS

Love you today, love you today,
the hell with tomorrow they can't pry me away.
I'll pull you closer as the clock ticks away.
Look in my eyes . . . . I'll love you today.

I know you'll go back to him who won't treat you right,
and I'll lay on the edge of my bed and sleep restless tonight.
As I look on the calendar at our upcoming windows of time,
it's never enough but those hours I know that you're mine.

Love you today, love you today,
the hell with tomorrow they can't pry me away.
I'll pull you closer as the clock ticks away.
Look in my eyes . . . . I'll love you today.

ACKNOWLEDGMENTS

Thanks to tatlin.net for the wonderful cover that captures the essence of the book

Thanks to Jill Hartman-Roberts who did a spectacular job editing many of the chapters of this book

Thanks to the other members of the AWA who helped edit and shape the book including Zhanna, Jennifer, Sharon, Charlie and Nancy.

Thanks to all of those people whose names I cannot mention for their story contributions. Without all of you there would be no book.

Thanks to you for spending your hard earned money on this book.

`Brad Rudisail

Introduction

In my previous book, *Someday I'm Going To*, I introduced a man named Gus who told the tale of his personal quest to capture the heart of his newly discovered true love, hoping they'd be together forever.

I met Gus for the first time when I interviewed him. I have never forgotten him. His story haunted me for months after our meeting. I still get misty eyed at times thinking about his story. Here was a man who sacrificed everything, all for the love of a woman named Lisa. Gus was so moved by retelling his own story that he was compelled to stop in the middle of our interview as the tears began falling more easily than his words flowed. As I have also included Gus's story in this book, I do not want to give away too much before you have had a chance to read it for yourself.

This was not my first encounter with someone whose life changed forever as a result of an extramarital relationship. Three years before I met Gus, I watched my friend, Justin, virtually transform in front of my eyes thanks to his affair with a woman who gave him the love and esteem he had long been lacking in his life. Given his horrible marriage and horrible life overall, his phenomenal metamorphosis was nothing short of miraculous, something that I duly noted for future reference.

It was ultimately these two profoundly inspiring stories that propelled me to write about the taboo subject of extramarital affairs. As a writer, I find this proscribed topic to be exceptionally fertile ground, containing all of the necessary ingredients of a sure-fire recipe for inquisitive reading: love, joy, ecstasy, tranquility, escapism, betrayal, heartbreak, stress and despondency. With all of those emotions dished out in large quantities, these infidelities make up the very essence of human drama.

Initially, I had doubts about whether or not I would find enough people with comparable experiences to Gus's and Justin's who would be willing to share the stories I needed to fill the pages of this book. To my complete surprise, I had little difficulty finding an ample supply of willing participants with analogous experiences to divulge. Though my good luck made the realization of this book far easier than I anticipated, it also leads me to conclude that sadly there are so many unhappily married people living among us.

You may be curious as to why someone would divulge such taboo secrets to a stranger. Several of these individuals told me that I was the first person to whom they had ever disclosed their experiences. Some said it was therapeutic for them to finally reveal their double lives to someone. On the other hand, many of the individuals discussed in this book may never retain a copy of it for fear of risk of exposure.

My intent from the beginning was to include an equal representation of men and women in this compilation of true stories; although, I was certain that I would end up short on my quota of female contributors. I could not have been more wrong. In fact, I received a plethora of responses from women eager to spew all of the details surrounding their clandestine romances. As it turned out, I had to deliberately pick and choose which women's tales to include in this book based on my overall goal and to balance out the content as a whole. From my experience with both men and women that I interviewed, I surprisingly found that in general the women were far more open to discussing this subject than the men were. I also came to the following conclusion, which validated a long-standing assumption of mine: that extramarital relationships are not necessarily a male dominated experience, but are most definitely a human one.

As the author and objective witness to these testimonials, I neither condone, nor condemn, the actions of the people whose private lives are revealed in this written work. However, I found every one of these people to be compelling individuals with open hearts despairing from an emptiness buried deep within. They are ordinary people, attempting to live out their lives as best as they can with the cards life has dealt them, cards that left them with large voids in their personal lives. I will leave it up to you, the reader, to judge whether or not their human need to fill that void justifies the choices they made.

Everyone featured in this book is a real person; although, I have altered their names in order to protect their identities. One of the last people I interviewed was a man named Patrick. It was Patrick who first used the term: 'The Game.' It is a perfect classification of the calculated maneuvers in which these lovers engage and the subsequent anxieties they willingly endure to play 'The Game.' I was so gripped by Patrick's insightful label that I chose to base the title of this book around that concept and to open the book with his story. However, as aptly as Patrick's metaphor captures the adventure of the extramarital lifestyle, I've come to the conclusion that these narratives are much more than just enticing drama. Woven into the fabric of these true stories lies the revelation that the quest to find love never dies. It is inherent in all of us: man and woman, rich and poor, black and white, and yes, single and married. What truly makes these illicit affairs so addictive and seductive, in my view, is that inherent, yet elusive, focus on living in the present moment. The two lovers, forced to remain apart, are only allotted narrow windows of time to be together. Because of that foreboding clock, nothing is ever taken for granted. Every moment is precious. Every conversation is enjoyed. Every kind act is acknowledged. Every kiss is relished. To use my previous book as a comparison, the participants in an extramarital affair are not consumed with 'Someday.' All that matters to them is 'the Now.' In the end, they cannot help themselves. They are driven to seek out more for themselves than what their marriages offer them. And in doing so, they are helpless to resist the urge to engage in this 'Game' of forbidden love.

DEDICATION

This book is dedicated to all of those who are hurting and searching diligently for love.

`Brad Rudisail

The Game

Play, play the game tonight
Can you tell me if it's wrong or right
Is it worth the time, is it worth the price
Do you see yourself in the white spotlight
Then play the game tonight

- Kansas, Play the Game Tonight

As Patrick sat in his counselor's office she asked him, "Patrick, do you ever think of killing yourself?"

"No, of course not," he replied, "but if I were to be hit by a bus this afternoon, at least 'The Game' would be over, which isn't a bad thing." He paused, waiting for her reaction. "At least your thoughts of death are only passive in nature," she responded as she hurriedly added to her notes on the memo pad residing on her lap.

Those who have been deeply involved in an extramarital love relationship undoubtedly know the game of which I speak. For those of you who have never dipped your toe into such treacherous waters, you have no earthly clue what Patrick is talking about, or how he could even kid about being run over by a bus.

That's because you haven't played the game.

So what is the game?

"The game is something I wouldn't wish on my worst enemy," explains Patrick. "The game is a deadly mental foray of highs and lows, peaks and valleys, elation and anguish. It consumes your thoughts, your energies, and if you don't watch it, your very soul."

"The game is laying on your couch on Christmas Eve, wondering if she is with "him" beside the tree in the living room, and wondering if he bought her an expensive gift, perhaps an elegant tennis bracelet, in a last ditch attempt to win her back.

"The game is running into her in a public place, surrounded by people who know us, but don't know *of* us, forcing us to maintain our charade that we aren't a couple at all.

"The game is sitting in your office, while she visits her mom and relatives in her hometown, wondering to yourself if you will ever meet her family, and wondering if her mother and siblings will ever learn about you and how much you love her.

"The game is playing out the charade of your own domestic role at home, while all you can think about is being with her, at her house - as her husband.

"The game is not being able to sleep every other night, as you lie awake wondering if she will ever really leave him.

"The game is about juggling double lives and keeping track of all the stories and the lies. It is exhausting to keep track of it all, not to mention the constant trips to the other side of town to see her whenever the opportunity presents itself.

"The game is about the ominous, ever-present clock. Similar to the games played in professional sports, this game is also managed by a clock that monitors the few precious minutes you can spend with her as it ticks by ever so quickly.

And yet, like so many others, Patrick is willing to play this game in order to be with that one person in the world who captures his heart like no other woman in the world. Despite its often sinister nature, Patrick is willing to play the game because Kelly makes his heart smile in a manner it had never smiled before. Despite the deleterious corollaries of the game, her enduring love has sprouted dreams within him, and her perpetual adoration for him is fertilizing those dreams even now. He is convinced that today's dreams will evolve into tomorrow's realities.

I thought back to an interview I had done several months ago in which a lady put it best when she divulged to me that she had been in an affair for just over two years. Both of them were merely seeking a temporary oasis to escape the day-to-day involvement of a bad marriage at the time they met. Upon meeting each other however, they felt an immediate attraction to one another, which was the seed that quickly grew into a deep devotional love for one another. After fourteen months they realized both wanted to spend the rest of their lives together and decided to leave their spouses and eventually marry. They both vowed to leave simultaneously so one would not be stuck on the sidelines waiting for the other, but try as they might, they never could get it together. Finally after two years, they called it quits, not because they no longer loved each other, but because they were simply exhausted. The game does that, it wears you out at some point.

Patrick tells the story of how when Kelly begged him to meet her at a party that a friend of hers was hosting. It was only five months into their relationship, and they just couldn't see enough of each other. Although she was going alone, most of the people at the party knew her husband, so they wouldn't be free to outwardly show their intense interest in one another. It sounded thrilling, alluring and a little naughty, almost like they were starring in a short film about the sexy ruse they planned to pull off while mingling with the other party guests. The reality fell far short of that; however, as they spent much of the party on opposite sides of every room they both happened to occupy. Even worse, Patrick had to watch other husbands vivaciously flirt with Kelly, which apparently was the protocol at this party. After two hours, he had suffered through enough, and he quietly left the party. Kelly also snuck outside, without anyone noticing, and Patrick told her what a truly stupid idea it had been.

"We've pushed the envelope much further than you could ever imagine," he confessed to the counselor.

"We've been to parties together, gone out to dinner in public places just blocks from each of our homes. I even helped her celebrate her son's birthday one night when the deadbeat father was out of town."

"Goodness, that is so unhealthy," exclaimed the therapist. "Please tell me the two of you aren't doing anything like that anymore."

"We're not," he answered assumingly. "I finally told Kelly I wasn't going to be with her in any environment in which we couldn't be a public couple."

"Thank goodness," she replied.

Thank goodness indeed. Ten months into their relationship, he politely asked Kelly to no longer tell him what she was doing on week nights or weekends. Ignorance is bliss when your heart aches to be with someone who is married to someone else. He didn't want to know what she was cooking for dinner for her family because he would want to sit at the dinner table with her and her son to enjoy her culinary delicacies. He didn't want to know when she was going to a party because he would yearn to accompany her. He didn't want to know if she was meeting a friend for a drink because he so desperately desired to meet all of her friends and have them witness his fully committed love for Kelly.

Patrick has never forgotten the time when she returned to her hometown to mourn her father's death. Her asshole husband didn't even bother to show up, didn't even call or send a card. He longed to stand beside her, holding her hand, supporting her and protecting her. He longed to honor the man who had helped raise the woman of my dreams and silently thank him as they lowered his coffin into the grave. He longed to meet the mother who brought her into this world. He longed to convey his condolences to all of her family and demonstrate that he could take on the role of the strong, supportive and loving husband that had been absent from her life for so long. Instead however, Patrick remained two thousand miles away, as he would the following Christmas, when Kelly returned home yet again.

"You look forward to holidays and special moments when you're in a 'normal' relationship," says Patrick. "Not so if you are having an affair. You don't get to attend a Super Bowl party together. You don't get to share one another's birthdays on the actual date. Holidays are totally out of the question. You never get to see each other's church, favorite neighborhood bar or regular hangout. You don't get to attend their kid's basketball game. You are always restricted to remain on the outside."

"I told my counselor that some days I don't know what's real and what isn't. I just don't know what is, and what and isn't, part of the charade. Is the charade my running through the motions of my current domestic life, or is the notion that Kelly and I will end up as a real couple one day the real charade? I just don't know anymore."

No he doesn't. It's hard to know what to do some days. He has met Kelly's son. He is a wonderful boy but because of a father who has no time for him, he is a shell of the young man he could be at the age of sixteen. Patrick would love the opportunity to toss the ball back and forth with him since he never experienced that with his father. He has to hold his tongue and not scold him when he emulates his father and totally disrespects his mother. Patrick would love to take he and his mother on a trip and show him what's it's like to be in a true family environment, but he can't. Unfortunately he can't make an impact on him and risk his mentioning it in front of his dad.

Patrick is fully aware of how uncomfortable, and even scary, it will be for Kelly to tell her husband she wants to leave him. As the man who loves her more than any woman he has ever loved before, he doesn't want her to endure the hardship of leaving him, and in a sense he feels like he should simply accept the small windows of time that he is blessed to be spending with her. Yet, at the same time, he feels that the level of commitment and dedication that he has shown her deserves something more than the crumbs that he is allotted. The game is affecting his mental state, and even his physical health too. He knows she witnesses the manner in which the game is negatively impacting him, and feels that if she truly loves him as much as she states, she would want to take that uncomfortable, scary step that he wishes for her to take every day of his life.

"Patrick, you said you approached your wife recently

about leaving her a year or so ago but you hesitated to pull the trigger completely on divorcing her," said the counselor. "Why haven't you simply left her?"

"My wife is in no hurry to end our marriage. She enjoys the gravy train that I provide her," he answered. "And if I were to leave her, then what? I'd sit in an apartment every Friday and Saturday night wanting to be with my girlfriend, like any other single guy out there, except, of course, I can't because my girlfriend is married to another man. Then I would really lose my mind. I don't want to be a single man chasing a married woman for the rest of my life. She and I have taken this journey together so far, and we need to take that big step together as well. If I am to love her, better I love her shackled to the same extent as she is."

The counselor processed Patrick's last statement and answered, "I agree, you certainly couldn't handle that situation." Have you ever thought of leaving both of them? What's the job market like in your field? Would it be easy for you to relocate to another city and start over again? There are many single women out there who would be thrilled to be Mrs. Patrick and they wouldn't have to leave a husband to do it."

"Yes, I have thought of that," he answered.

In fact, Patrick has thought of every possible course of action imaginable. He gave her a deadline on Thanksgiving night. It was their third Thanksgiving since they had met. Actually it wasn't "their" Thanksgiving, none of them were "theirs" because they weren't together for any of them. The previous two Thanksgivings, she'd accompanied her husband out of state to spend the holiday week with his family. This year she'd told her husband that she was not going to travel with him, so he invited his siblings and their families to spend Thanksgiving at their home. This of course meant that Kelly would be preparing Thanksgiving dinner for all of them. Why of course would one go to all of that trouble if they were simply going to leave? After a heart wrenching holiday that Thursday, Patrick texted her that night and informed her she had one week to tell him she wanted to leave or I would end our affair. He said that he would do the same with his wife as well, and implore that she see an attorney, which he did.

The good news was that she woke up the following morning and told her husband she wanted out of their marriage. The bad news was that after a short fifteen minute conversation, he simply walked away and ignored both her and the issue. The two of them then spent the next four weeks acting as if the subject had never been brought up. They were ignoring their reality.

Her husband had actually been putting in a trickle of effort to repair their marriage since their brief conversation, which is why on Christmas Eve night, Patrick was sprawled out on the guest bed with tears streaming from my eyes, thinking about her, her mom, her son and "him", gathered around the family room, enjoying themselves. He said he would have proposed to her beside their tree on Christmas Eve if he and Kelly were a "normal" couple. Her mom would have sat quietly on the couch, her eyes tearing up with joy, fully aware of his love for Kelly by now and how much I made her daughter's heart smile. She despised her so-called son-in-law since he'd committed the unforgivable sin of avoiding her own husband's funeral.

"But it wasn't meant to be, because on holidays, I am the 'affair guy,'" says Patrick. "I am the guy sentenced to the outside of the home, forced to only observe through the steamed up windowpanes. I was certain that her husband was on his best behavior, playing out his own charade in an attempt to win back the favor of his wife and mother-in-law. I began imagining every worst-case scenario in my mind. I felt so alone. I know now why Christmas can be the loneliest time of the year."

"The following day I drove my own mother back to her house, just after a noontime Christmas dinner. We drove in silence for most of the ride, for I was exhausted both emotionally and physically, having only slept two hours the previous night. Shortly after dropping off my mom at home, I parked the car in an empty parking lot near her house and called Kelly. It was against game rules to call each other at home when the rest of the family was present. Neither of us had ever broken protocol before, but today I did not care. I called and texted repeatedly, even leaving a desperate voice mail. She finally texted back that she would call me back, which she did.

"I can't go on like this," I cried to her, "this not knowing, this perpetual feeling of not knowing if and when we can ever be together. I want to be with you, not only for Christmas Day every year, but I want to be with you when you bake the Christmas cookies the week before too so I can sneak in kisses between each batch you make I want to carve the Thanksgiving Turkey with you, as well as the Christmas Ham, every year for the rest of my life. I want to be able to hold your hand no matter where we are, and sneak you a kiss no matter who is in our presence. I want it all Kelly. There are guys out there who don't give you much in a relationship, but they don't expect much in return either. Guys like me, we will give you the world, but at some point, we want it all, or we are willing to walk away with nothing. Today is the day for me, my love. Today is that day. Am I going to walk with you for the rest of my life, or walk away from you forever? In order for me to play the game for one more moment, your husband must play too, or I will take my ball and go home, never to see you again."

Two days after her mom returned home from the holiday vacation, Kelly approached her husband yet again. This time, however, she refused to let him escape in avoidance. She forced him to sit across from her for over two hours and listen as she clearly communicated her intentions. They did not break up that day, but he did shed a tear as he realized that his many years of neglecting his wife and family, his many years of doling out verbal abuse, his many years of denying her the love and attention that every wife wants and deserves, had finally caught up with him. **That tear told him that he was now feeling the sting of the game,** and that was enough for Patrick for now.

Kelly vows to soon finish what she started that day, and Patrick once again has reason to dream of that day on the beach they so often talk about when he will slide another ring on her finger, a ring that will make her his wife, and be a sign of the lifetime commitment of love and devotion that he will pledge to her forever.

For a little bit longer, Patrick is going to play the game.

I Just Want to Be Lois Lane for a While

I am, I am, I am Superman
and I know what's happening.
I am, I am, I am Superman
and I can do anything.

-    *Superman*, REM

I interviewed Angela over a cup of coffee one morning. She represents so many women today who are overworked, over-committed and over-stressed. She is a giver, and the thing about giving all the time is that, eventually, you give out. I wish I had met her prior to the timetable of this story so that I could have witnessed the difference in her demeanor and personality before and after the relationships that gave her the much-needed escape she needed. This is her story:

"I was enjoying a lunch date with yet another man I had met on the Internet. He was my third lunch date this month as I was putting a lot of effort into meeting someone. He and I had really hit it off online. I had high hopes for this guy and me. We had spoken on the phone a couple of times prior to our first date, and his wit and charm were very enticing. His confidence and the way he spoke so eloquently excited me. However, this time, I was doing most of the talking so far, somewhat out of nervousness I guess, and also because I needed to rant a little bit.. He was making even more headway with me in person due to the fact that, unlike my husband of seventeen years, he was intently listening to my every word and displayed apparent interest, whether or not it was genuine.

"I was describing a typical week in the life of Angela to him. I have a very demanding job in the finance department of a large hospital that often requires me to take work home with me. I am also the mother of two very athletic boys, which requires me to transport them to all of their games and practices. On top of that, I have a husband who does absolutely nothing around the house to help out, which means that I end up doing all of the cooking, cleaning and even home repair, believe it or not. As I was recounting my busy life to him, I began to wonder how in the world I had time for a romantic relationship on top of everything else since I barely had any time for myself. I imagined he must have been thinking the same thing.

"'I get it,' he said after I had finally paused long enough for him to get a word in edgewise. "You're tired of being Superman all the time for your family and now you want to just be Lois Lane for a while.

"I think my jaw dropped upon hearing him say that. He had just articulated the summation of my feelings in one simple phrase. Yes, I was tired of being Superman, tired of being the super hero that my family constantly depended on without a respite. I definitely wanted to be

Lois Lane for a while. I wanted to be the damsel in distress and let Superman come to my rescue. I wanted a man to wine and dine me and woo me into bed. I wanted him to take me and make love to me again and again. I wanted someone to take over being in charge, instead of the other way around, like my life had been for over a decade. This guy got it. He understood where I was coming from. He understood me.

"We talked nonstop for the full duration of lunch. He picked up the tab without hesitation, which impressed me, and then we both headed for the door. I pointed to my van parked in the front row of the restaurant parking lot. Being that I wanted a goodbye kiss, I was wishing that I had parked in a less conspicuous spot. He walked me up to the driver's door, thanked me for lunch and then leaned forward to kiss me. The moment our lips touched, we pulled each other in, our arms wrapped around each other in lockstep. My God, he knew how to kiss! And then, as quickly as the storm within us had brewed, it dissipated again as we caught ourselves, realizing that we were putting on a show for everyone in sight.

"I drove back to work, but I couldn't concentrate-not for a minute. I was thinking about his Lois Lane comment and that incredible kiss. I couldn't wait to see him again. It wasn't in my nature to just hop in bed with a man I barely knew; yet, that night I couldn't stop thinking about him. I kept wishing he were there beside me, putting forth his best moves to seduce me, which I knew he could do so easily. Doubting my own sex appeal, I felt like he was totally out of my league. As far as I was concerned, he could be any woman's Superman. I wanted him to be mine.

"My husband and I had ceased being intimate years ago. I thought men always wanted sex, but he seemed to have lost all of his sex drive-at least when it came to me. I have to take on some of the blame for it, because due to my hectic schedule, I had let myself go over the years with a poor diet and lack of exercise. I was also in dire need of a makeover. I don't even remember the last time I had my hair done at a salon. I've sometimes wondered if he was having an affair, or if he looked for intimacy elsewhere as well, but I always dismissed the idea. I don't think he has it in him to cheat.

"We met again the next week for lunch. I told him I couldn't stray far from the hospital that week because of an audit that was due, and I suggested that we have lunch in a park just a couple of miles from the hospital. He said he would take care of everything, which he did immaculately. We did the blanket thing with dainty sandwiches he had picked up from a deli nearby as well as various fruits and chocolate covered strawberries. He had even scouted out a somewhat secluded spot for us. It was perfect.

"He was so cute in that he kept inching closer to me as we ate until, by the time we had consumed everything he brought, he was sitting right up against me. He reached out to offer me a kiss, which I readily accepted. We began making out right there in the park. As our kisses grew deeper and more passionate, his hands began roaming my body. Soon I felt his hand cupping one of my breasts through my blouse. From there, his hand made its way down my body to my legs where he began exploring my thighs underneath my skirt. I couldn't believe what he was doing! I was worried to death that someone was watching us. He soon began gracefully caressing me across my panties. I wanted him to touch me for real so badly, and he didn't disappoint. We were still kissing each other deeply as I felt myself climaxing into orgasm. I stifled my screams of elation against his muscular chest.

"A full minute passed by in silence as I was left speechless from our public display. I'm sure he was expecting me to reciprocate, but I couldn't muster up the gumption to do anything further right there in the park. All I could say was, 'I need to get back to work dear before they start to wonder about me.'

"I could tell he was a little disappointed. We folded up the blanket, scooped up our trash and began strolling hand in hand through the park back to the parking lot. As we made our way onto the sidewalk I found myself saying: 'tell you what, I can be a little late today. Why don't we get into my van and park it in a more isolated area and let me have my way with you, dear?' I was expecting to hear a resounding 'yes' come from his mouth, but instead he let go of my hand and began quickly walking ahead of me, scooting past another young, romantic couple approaching us from the opposite direction.

"I wasn't sure if it was something I said, or if he was upset about my earlier display of shyness and never heard my sexual proposition. I eventually found him, standing propped up against my van. He looked pale as if he had just seen a ghost, and beads of sweat were dripping from his brow. He leaned over and told me that the girl in the pair approaching us when he left was his wife's niece, and that she had seen us holding hands. I could tell he was spooked and was shooting straight with me. He said he had to go, and we parted ways quietly, trying not to bring anymore unwanted attention to ourselves.

"I didn't hear from him for two days. He said that the niece had called his wife, but that things weren't as bad as he thought they might be, and that once things quieted down in a couple of weeks, he wanted to see me again. The last thing I wanted to deal with was the threat of an angry wife calling my house or knocking on my door one day, so I told him that I couldn't risk that possibility. I told him we couldn't see each other again. He said he understood and wished me the best, thanking me for the time we had shared together.

"I still think about that day and the 'what if's' that might have occurred between my Superman and me. We were clearly in the wrong place at the wrong time that day. What were the odds of a family member being at the park that day? What a pity!

"I did eventually meet a nice man online whom I have had a relationship with for the past six months, and we are very content together. My newfound relationship has made me much happier and rendered my situation more tolerable. I don't see myself ever divorcing my husband for my boyfriend, but you never know. I might not be with Superman today, but I certainly feel more like Lois Lane these days."

Three Months of Heaven for Justin

John Kinsella: *Is this heaven?*
Ray Kinsella: *It's Iowa.*
John Kinsella: *Iowa? I could have sworn this was heaven.*
[*John starts to walk away*]
Ray Kinsella: *Is there a heaven?*
John Kinsella: *Oh yeah. It's the place where dreams come true.*

-     *Field of Dreams*

It was on a cold day in February, standing behind a bunch of noisy servers in a data center, that I received a continuing stream of text messages on my Blackberry from a buddy of mine I used to work with named Justin.

Like me, Justin was lost in his early teenage years and was the victim of trying too hard to fit in with the crowd. He had always been somewhat of a lost soul. Like me, work consumed much of his energy and time.   After stumbling around in his twenties, he discovered that he held the skills required to be a successful salesperson who could connect with customers on a personal level.   He also became a budding entrepreneur and created many sideline opportunities for himself. He has a ton of energy and likes to be the life of the party if he has time to attend it.

On that cold day in February, Justin began bombarding my Blackberry with a flurry of text messages and pictures of a stunning woman who had totally captured his heart. I spent much of that day absorbed in his tales of Jessica. It's a hell of a feeling witnessing total joy emanating from another human being. Every word, texted or spoken, encapsulated complete and total exhilaration that day. I began to wonder if I had ever been that excited about something in my life. What I was witnessing was the total transformation of my friend, and it is that event that would later serve as the fruition of this book. This is Justin's story in his own words:

"Love finds you when you least expect it. I got married at age 31, late for a first marriage, but I never felt like taking that step until I met my ex-wife. Up to that point, I had really never enjoyed a long-term relationship, but rather had endured a love life that never seemed to get off the ground. My dating life was simply a series of eternal breakups. Rather than hearing those words, 'I do', I was always hearing the words, 'You're a nice guy Justin, but...' If you're honest with yourself, after a while you'll finally confess to the fact that you're partly to blame for reliving the same script over and over again, and you'll learn how to move on. I realized that I had low self-esteem for years due to having a mentally and physically abusive stepmother growing up. In my late twenties, I finally took charge of my life, distancing myself from the oppression of my childhood, and I found out that life becomes a hell of a lot happier when you're happy inside first.

"It was at that point that I met my wife-to-be. She was divorced with three young children. I remember friends and family asking me if I was sure I wanted to date someone with children. She was attractive, outgoing and the opposite of anyone I had ever dated. After two and a-half years of dating, we married, and I finally heard that wondrous phrase, 'I do'. I was happy and had three great kids and a wife whom I believed truly loved me. We seemed like that perfect little family in the beautiful house in the suburbs.

"Shortly after we got married, I got a great sales job and bought her a brand new car, keeping a used one for my own needs. Her two sons wanted to play hockey, and I gladly paid for all of his equipment, skating lessons, travel expenses and everything else that goes with it. Her daughter was also a good athlete. Softball was her specialty and I gladly paid for us to fly to tournaments across the country, even during a period in which I was unemployed and had to resort to fundraising. I gave to those kids as if they were my own, and everyone who met us simply assumed that I was their natural father.

"I was a giver. Everyone needs to be a giver, but after a while, givers need to receive as well in order to replenish themselves. I was busy playing the role of the provider, working as many as three jobs at one time. I soon discovered my wife had credit cards I never knew about, and I began to find merchandise in secretive places throughout the house. It all made me feel like an outsider. It was more than the money, though. I had made other types of sacrifices for years, such as the attendance of events with my side of the family, as well as with my friends, and it all seemed for naught. I felt unappreciated and unloved.

"Our marriage had lacked all signs of intimacy for seven years. Like other lonely married people, I turned to the Internet and built a nice camaraderie with some wonderful women. Unfortunately, none of them lived near me, but my late night conversations with them helped to fill the emptiness at home. In the end, though, I still lacked the physical connection--the human touch and the feeling of being loved or wanted. All through that period, I stayed true to my Catholic upbringing and never strayed or cheated on my wife. It was then that I began to once again turn to the crux of my childhood, thinking that happiness just wasn't in the cards for me.

"And then one afternoon, it happened.

"I was at a local tavern enjoying a cold beer when I heard an Australian accent over my shoulder. I turned to look, and it was then that I saw the most beautiful woman, with eyes unlike any I had ever seen. I had to say something, but the best I could come up with was:

'Love your accent. Where in Australia are you from?' She responded to my lame attempt at coming on to her by saying that Australians don't have an accent but that ours is quite cute. We shared a laugh, and then we shared five hours of conversation over three bottles of wine. I felt twenty years younger talking to her, I guess partly because she was roughly twenty years younger than I was. She told me her name was Jessica, and I found out she was going to be here for three months, which immediately made me hope I would run into her again. At the end of the day, I walked Jessica to her car, gave her a hug goodbye, and as I was leaving, I heard her say, 'Thank you, Justin, for a wonderful evening.' I was smiling while walking to my car, but then kicked myself as I opened the car door as I realized I hadn't gotten her number nor given her mine.

"Later that night, I hopped into the refuge of a hot shower--a place I often escaped to within my house-- and replayed the series of events of the day. As I exited the shower, my phone vibrated, and upon checking it, I discovered four texts from a number I didn't recognize. As I curiously opened the first text, I saw the name displayed in written form on my screen. It was my new favorite name: Jessica. All four texts were further confirmations of how much she had enjoyed both the evening and my company.

"I answered, replying to her text messages after rereading them several times. I asked how she got my number, and she said that she had called the bar and gotten it from the owner. That night, I voluntarily slept on the couch and texted Jessica into the wee hours of the night.

"The next morning, the sound of my phone vibrating woke me up. I looked down and saw a text saying: 'Good morning, Sunshine, have a great day! – Jessica.' As the morning went on, taking me from sales call to sales call, I found myself totally transfixed by her. She called me just prior to lunch and asked if I could join her. I did, and once again, I couldn't leave the table. I set up a temporary office right there on the spot, calling my accounts in between our lines of conversation. We ended up remaining at that table until damn near dinnertime, and if I hadn't had to go home that evening, we may have closed the place. I explained to her I had to go home, and she said she understood, and that she wasn't looking for a relationship, or to create a moment that would come between my wife and me. For the rest of her time in town, it was assumed we would be very good friends. I hugged her goodbye. I certainly didn't want to hear the 'friend' line again, but I knew that realistically someone her age was not going to fall for a married suburbanite in his late forties. But hey, a guy can dream.

"That lunch date evolved into a routine we both looked forward to several times a week. Thanks to my job, I knew all the best places to eat, and she was enjoying our culinary tour across the city. One morning, she called me and said she wanted to break the routine and have me over and fix me lunch. It was a thrill watching her prepare our meal and being in her personal living space. She asked if I had time to hang out that afternoon and watch movies on the couch. 'Sure!' I exclaimed, as I proceeded to call from her bathroom to postpone my next appointment until the next day.

"As we started to watch the movie, she took my hand--not as a friend, but as a stimulated woman. She leaned against me and said, 'I want to be more than just friends.' There's always a kiss that follows a moment like that, and I can tell you that it contained all the fireworks it was supposed to. The couch later led to the bed, which led to me not leaving her side until almost 1 a.m. The drive home that night was confusing for me. This was the first time I had ever cheated on my wife, yet being with Jessie felt like the most comfortable yet fulfilling thing I had done in years.

"I found myself spending every possible moment with Jessica, and those moments culminated quickly into my falling in love with her. We shared laughter and conversation every day--not to mention the most incredible sex of my life, which sometimes included carrying out unfulfilled fantasies and sexual exploits. One afternoon while we were out walking and holding hands, she looked at me with tears in her eyes and informed me she soon would be going back to Australia. She wanted us to spend her last weekend together so that we could share every moment. I called a friend of mine who said he would cover for me, and I went on to spend the most incredible weekend of my life. Never had I craved someone as much as I did her. It was one of those clothing-optional weekends, during which we barely left each other's side.

"The hardest day of my life was the day I drove her to the airport. We both cried like babies and fought to gather our composure, only to cry again in each other's arms. Jessica made me feel wanted and attractive for the first time in my life. I no longer felt alone. She showed me love and compassion and made me realize I am a great guy with a lot to offer someone. Shortly after her departure, I filed for divorce, and my wife and I parted in an amicable manner.

"Jessica and I still keep in touch, and who knows if we will ever end up together. I plan on visiting Australia later this year to see the land where she came from, if nothing else. I long to hold and kiss her again, but most of all I long to tell her that she taught me how to fall in love again. I would love to plan a life with Jessica in her native land. I have nothing holding me here presently. I could easily see myself spending the rest of my life with her. I know this may be a pipe dream, but dreams are what get you through a bad reality.

"In case I don't get to live out my dream, I know the confidence that Jessica gave me will make me more desirable to someone else. I would like to marry again, and if it happens with someone other than Jessica, then my future wife will also have her to thank, for Jessica transformed me into a man who knows how to love."

Big John

Every morning at the mine you could see him arrive.
He stood six-foot-six and weighed two-forty-five.
Kinda broad at the shoulder and narrow at the hip.
Everybody knew you didn't give no lip to Big John.

- Johnny Cash, *Big John*

One of the plights of the male when it comes to romance is that he traditionally is the one who must throw himself out there. The pressure falls on him whether he's working up the nerve to ask that girl in the school hallway if she's going to the dance, or whether he's frantically rehearsing his opening lines as he waits for her to pick up her cell phone so he may ask her out this weekend. It's also customary for the man to ask the woman for her hand in marriage. We all love to hear those stories of a man proposing to the woman with whom he wants to spend the rest of his life. We love those stories, not just because they drip with romance, but also because we watch these romantic life skits with bated breath as we await her answer. There are never any guarantees when it comes to love, and many a guy has had his heart ripped out as a result of a wedding proposition.

The same applies when exiting a relationship in the name of love: **often the responsibility falls upon the man**. When two people in love, married to other people, are ready to leave their respective spouses to pursue a new life together, one of the parties must take the lead. Although I don't think there are any established protocols when it comes to affairs, it does seem that there is an expectation that the man should take the initiative and dramatically change his world. As noted earlier in the book, this means that even though he is a free man, he must continue to live constricted within the confines of marriage boundaries, and he must do something that is very difficult: He must wait for her to leave her spouse, which sometimes is the hardest thing to do.

This plight is emphasized in a story told by a lady named Grace. Although I had already included a similar story in the book, I was enthralled by her narration. Grace tells it best.

"My name is Grace, and I had two affairs during the final years of my marriage. I am not ashamed of the affairs I had. I was in a very abusive relationship, one in which my husband constantly battered me, not physically, but emotionally and verbally. I found that an abusive relationship is like a hole you've dug with your partner. Every abusive incident, every guilty thought, every humiliation and every reconciliation digs the hole just that much deeper. The only people who are truly privy to the depths of that hole are you and your partner. No one else understands why you stay in the hole, but the hole is yours. Leaving that hole is so hard, in part because you have no idea what your life could possibly look like outside of the hole. It is extremely scary, and because of that, leaving that hole is something folks rarely do.

"I managed to do it though, thanks to the gentlemen with whom I had relations. These weren't sexual affairs per se. These were men who complimented me often, cared about me, appreciated my strengths and looked past my weaknesses. They also loved the woman within me. They desired me physically, something my husband hadn't done in a decade. Every loving act of kindness, thoughtfulness, and compassion, every compliment or desirous comment, helped fill in that hole just a little bit more each time, such that one day I was able to simply walk out of that hole. Affairs were my ticket to imagining new realities, while I gathered the strength to finally leave my husband, which I did of my own volition.

"As soon as I left my husband, all of my friends wanted to set me up with men; of course, they didn't know I had been seeing other men over the past several years. One of my friends, Todd, told me about another friend of his named John. He said John had left his wife the year before and was having trouble getting back in the game. He humorously told me that John needed to get laid, and that I did too, so we would probably be what each other needed.

"I agreed to go out with John, and when I met him, I

was glad I did. John was a big guy, broad shouldered, muscular and very tall. He could have been an offensive lineman in the NFL. His stature was unlike that of any other man I had been with, so I was OK with the idea of going out with him. He was the manager of a nearby paper mill and had a lot of responsibility. We had lunch the day I met him, which resulted in a dinner date that weekend, which then led to a second dinner date that concluded with a wonderful make out session in his SUV. He turned me on that night, and I was so looking forward to the time when he would wrap those big arms around me and pull me into his body.

"I got my opportunity the very next weekend. We spent much of the afternoon at a local arts festival and then shared a light dinner with drinks at a nearby café. Maybe it was the drinks, but I found myself asking him if he wanted to take me home and share a bottle of wine that I had been dying to open. He readily agreed.

"He uncorked the wine for me with an ease that I had not witnessed from any other man. We sat on the couch, with wine glasses in hand, and chatted as I waited for him to make a move on me. He finally did make his move, and we set down the wine glasses for what I hoped would be the rest of the night, anticipating that our hands would be occupied with each other. We began French kissing and groping each other. Somewhere amid our heavy breathing and moans of desire, I suggested we move ourselves to the bedroom. I told him to wait for me on the bed while I went to the bathroom to spruce up a bit.

"I had anticipated the evening going this way, which is why I wore my sexiest black bra and matching panties. As I undressed in front of the mirror, I imagined how he might look at me as I approached him. I wanted to sense his desire, and I anticipated him touching me. I was fully ready for this big brawny man to have his way with me as I opened my master bathroom door to make my way to the bed and fall into his arms.

"I expected to see John naked on the bed, totally aroused and waiting for me. Instead, I saw a crying man sitting on the edge of the bed. Immediately, my insecurities kicked in, and I was thinking that I had hit an all-time low by making a man cry at the thought of having sex with me. He immediately said it wasn't me. I sat down beside him. He apologized for breaking down and said he couldn't go through with it. Once he was able to cease sobbing, he told me that he'd had an affair with a lady named Amy during the last two years of a miserable marriage. Amy was also married, and she and her husband lived next door to John and his wife of thirty-three years. Amy and John both longed to be together full time. The plan was for John to leave his spouse first, which he did nineteen months ago. He waited patiently for eighteen months for Amy to make her move, only to hear her declare in the end that she wasn't going to leave her husband after all. He was devastated.

"As John told me this, I wanted to smack my stupid friend Todd in the face for bringing the two of us together. John's pain wasn't going to be alleviated by a few hours of sex. He was feeling the full impact of a broken heart, as well as the embarrassment of dramatically altering his life for nothing. John wasn't ready to go to bed with anyone. He was an emotional wreck.

"I stayed with John for a couple more hours, and we shared our stories. After that night, I never heard from him again. Last I heard from Todd was that John and Amy were once again seeing each other and were carrying on their relationship within the confines of her marriage.

"Yes, grown men cry, even men as big and manly as John. Managing relationships outside of one's marriage is difficult, and everyone gets hurt in some way unless he or she is just a cold-hearted son of a bitch. Eventually I married again, and somehow I still ended up with an abusive man. One night my second husband struck me. That time, however, I had the courage to leave immediately. I am a stronger person now, thanks to my experiences. I hope John is strong enough to sort out his future with Amy.

Expected to take the lead in love relationships, men often get their hearts stepped on by taking that first leap of faith. In John's case, his life was turned upside down when Amy crushed his hopes by not following through on her end after he took the initiative to leave his wife for her. The line, the bigger they are, the harder they fall, holds true for Big John.

I Always Cried Driving Home

She wonders how it ever got this crazy
She thinks about a boy she knew in school
Did she get tired or did she just get lazy?
She's so far gone she feels just like a fool

\-   Eagles, Lying Eyes

I stated at the beginning of this book that some who read it will judge those whose stories I am telling. It's easy to judge other people, to think someone is less righteous than yourself, having no knowledge of their circumstances, temptations, motivations or sufferings. It's a lot tougher to judge yourself, to stand in the mirror and account for one's own actions. That is what Anne does. She is her own judge and jury, and she continues to condemn her past deeds that she now wishes she could negate.

Anne is thirty-two years old and has been married for thirteen years. She and her husband don't have any children, but "that's a whole 'nother' story" she says. They both have good careers, a nice house and a vacation home on top of that. "We have all the material things we could want, really," she says. "We have a lot of nice things, and we have had a pretty good life together."

Anne goes on, "We both work, but he puts in much longer hours than I do, and sometimes that's a problem for us. Well, for me, anyway. I hate eating dinner alone after going to the trouble of preparing a great meal. I know he works hard to provide for us and keep us in this lifestyle we've grown accustomed to, but I work also."

Anne and her husband met one summer just after high school while working summer jobs at a hotel. They dated and fell madly in love with each other. They loved, they talked, and most importantly, they dreamed. "We dreamed big," Anne says with a smile. They made a plan for their life and mapped out how to get there. The wind was at their backs, and their ship made its way, gliding effortless across the water. It was a great time for them. It's always fun to dream and set sail to the lands beyond the horizon.

But that was the spring and early summer of their relationship. Soon, the dog days of August arrived and life moved more slowly. As I like to say, reality came to roost. Then came the changing winds of autumn. "I don't know why, or how, or even when it happened exactly," says Anne, "but our relationship began changing, and it's never been the same. To the rest of the world we are a very happy couple, 'perfect' in almost every way. We even manage to convince ourselves that things are great most of the time."

In those days of spring, Anne said that she knew what her husband was thinking before he even said a word. Now, she has no idea what he thinks. Anne says she misses the little things, those seemingly trivial tokens of love that we laugh about when other people receive them, but treasure every single one when we get them from that special someone. She yearns for the days of silly notes, text messages, romantic dinners, surprise flowers and cuddling on the couch. Most of all, she misses the intense connection she once shared with him and the passionate lovemaking that ensued as a result of their craving for one another.

"We used to do all of that and more," states Anne. "Most of these kinds of things have stopped. Instead of cuddling on the sofa we sit in separate chairs, instead of holding each other in bed there is a body pillow between us. Instead of talking about our future together, we talk about work and careers." As I am listening to her, I can't help but feel sadness. The child in me, like all children, wants so badly to believe in Barbie and Ken. Maybe the concept of Barbie and Ken are only toys though, never flesh.

Anne said she tried to spice things up and keep the spark alive, but she just got tired of trying after a while. "I was the only one making the effort," said Anne. "We still have sex, of course, but it's very predictable and seems almost like a task that must be completed rather than looking at it as the truly enjoyable experience it once was for us. I know this happens to couples. I guess I just thought it would happen much later in life. I'm too young to feel this way."

Anne begins apologizing for rambling. She says in an affirmative tone that she isn't the kind of person to cheat or hide things from her husband. She says that living with the guilt has proved unbearable. She keeps it all tucked away, wrapped up in a secluded corner inside her, knowing that she can never share it with anyone, or it would destroy her life and her marriage. She states that I am the first person to ever hear about this experience, and probably the last.

"I've probably shared enough, and while everything I've said is true, I'm not trying to excuse my behavior," she says ruefully. "I have betrayed my best friend in life, and I will never forgive myself. I do hope to reach a point where I don't think of myself as a bad person every day for what I've done. I pray a lot and ask for God's forgiveness, although I don't deserve it."

I will let Anne take it from here.

"I met him four years ago, and I will call him Matt. Our meeting was purely by accident, literally. We were both backing out of our parking spaces at the same time and slammed into each other. Both vehicles experienced only minor damage, so we decide to exchange information. He told me that his son-in-law owned a body shop and could probably fix both our cars really cheap if I wanted to avoid going through the insurance company. I told him I would consider his offer and we went our separate ways.

"There's no denying the instant attraction we both felt. I swear I felt my hairs standing on edge, as there was so much electricity in the air. I can't explain it. It was nothing I had ever felt before, not to that degree anyway. I felt the butterflies that afternoon. And as they fluttered in the pit of my stomach, a warm tingling sensation began emerging from there, flowing through my body, rejuvenating parts of me that I thought would be forever desolate. I began driving around aimlessly, wondering if he felt the same electricity. A couple days passed, and I finally heard from him. He said he wanted to follow up and see if I decided to accept his offer or not. I hadn't done anything with the car yet. He said his son-in-law's name was Luke, and he gave me the number of his shop. I agreed to meet him there.

"He was there when I arrived, and I felt those same sensations again. I parked next to him, took a deep breath and worked up the courage to step out of the car and talk with him. He introduced me to Luke, who looked over my damage and gave me a number that sounded awfully good to me. He said he could start right then. It was at that point that Matt offered to buy me a cup of coffee across the street while Luke went to work.

"That was yet another juncture where I should have said no. You say to yourself that you aren't doing anything wrong, but each step gives you the momentum to take the next baby step. We drank coffee and engaged in the usual small talk that's typical of those types of places. I felt comfortable around him. We spent an hour or two there. As we walked back to the shop, he turned to me and said, 'I hope you don't think it's strange of me to say this, but your husband sure is lucky.' I was startled by his comment because it seemed to come out of nowhere. I thanked him, and I even giggled a little bit, something I hadn't done in years in front of a man. I thought my heart was going to beat out of its chest.

"I got back to my car and found it laying in pieces. I was told that Luke had to order a part that wouldn't be in until the next day so I'd have to leave my car overnight. Looking back, I should have called a taxi or something, but when Matt offered to give me a lift home, I readily accepted. As we were driving, he told me that he was serious about his statement earlier. As we passed each city block during our drive, I could feel the conflict building inside of me. Sensing the sexual tension starting to build, he placed his hand on my leg. That was more than innocent flirting. I knew that, but I couldn't move his hand away. I was so attracted to him, and was so deliciously turned on by what he was doing, that I wanted to climb on top of him right then and there. His hand glided over my leg lightly so that I could just barely feel him through my dress.

"His hand then made its way slowly up my inner thigh,

and he began to tell me how attractive he found me. I felt so desired at that moment. I had forgotten what it felt like long ago. He told me he wanted to make love to me. Like Luke's estimate, I accepted his offer without saying a word. My eyes gave him the confirmation he needed. He pulled into the first hotel we came to and checked us in as husband and wife. We didn't make love like a husband and wife though. Our animal attraction for one another drove us both into a passionate frenzy. Our lovemaking was steamy and hot, the kind you read about, but rarely experience.

"I completely lost myself in the moment, and admittedly had the most intense orgasms of my life. We continued to meet weekly for a while, and each time was amazing, but each time I would cry while driving back home. I knew I was doing something wrong, and so I broke it off.

"Unfortunately, you can never undo what's been done. The sex was amazing with Matt, but he is not my husband, and never could be. Marriage is a lifetime commitment, no matter what happens. I will have to live with the choices I've made forever haunting me."

We Broke Our Only Rule

Well we busted out of class
Had to get away from those fools
We learned more from a three-minute record
Baby, than we ever learned in school
Tonight I hear the neighborhood drummer sound
I can feel my heart begin to pound
You say you're tired and you just wanna close your eyes
And follow your dreams down

Well we made a promise we swore we'd always
remember
No retreat, baby, no surrender
Like soldiers in the winter's night with a vow to defend
No retreat, baby, no surrender

- Bruce Springsteen, *No Surrender*

"On my deathbed I will regret the things I didn't do, not the things I did . . ."

That is how Nick began his story. This guy gets it, I thought. He is one year older than me at forty-nine and, like myself, feels that life is passing him by. Perhaps he has come to the point at which he feels that there's more history in the rearview mirror than there is opportunity lying ahead on the horizon. Nick, like the rest of the people outlined in this book, realized he could no longer sit on the sidelines and so he set out to make a change in his life.

It sounds like a cliché, but it was sex that was the catalyst for Nick's affair. Nick said that sex was only a once- or twice-a-year event in his marriage for more than twenty years. "It wasn't my choice to have a sexless marriage," said Nick. "My wife made a proclamation to me in 1992 that she no longer needed sex. Her exact words were: 'I'm different than you, sex is not that important to me. It does not validate our marriage and I don't care if we ever have sex again. I need you to get to the point where you don't bother me about it. Don't ask me, don't touch me, just leave me alone, I need space.'

"She has always viewed sex as a chore in which her goal is to make me cum and get the process over with," Nick goes on. "Prior to my affair I had never had sex that lasted more than a few minutes."

It wasn't like that in the beginning for Nick. Twenty-eight years ago when he first met his wife, the two of them couldn't keep their hands off of each other. As time went on, the sex was much less frequent. On the rare occasion they had sex, it was always at her discretion and under her terms.

Their love life aside however, things were great

between the two of them. They each benefited from highly successful careers and money was rarely in short supply. They shared common interests, goals and retirement dreams. "We have always gotten along well together," said Nick. "She isn't the devil. I really loved her."

Twelve years into their marriage, his wife said she wanted a family and they had two kids. "I love my children and would not trade them for the world," vows Nick. "They are the light of my life and the center of my happiness. Having said that, having children with her was the biggest mistake of my life. It cemented our marriage, assuring that our dead, sexless, emotionless, intimacy-void relationship would continue. Marriages like mine are very lonely. It's not something you ever discuss with buddies over a beer. Over time, I just learned to accept my life as it was, playing the hand I was dealt."

Like many people, sex to Nick isn't merely about just being pleasured. It's about the experience of pleasuring your partner as well, receiving the confirmation that you know how to excite and satisfy that person who is the apple of your eye. It's about exploring the physicality of your partner, learning what stimulates and excites them. It's the practice of getting to know them in a way like no one else. Sex is just sex, but intimacy is a wonderful progression in which two people lovingly grow together.

"I wanted a loving relationship," said Nick. "I wanted

to experience the whole package, the passion, the kissing, the feeling of touching and being touched. I wanted a woman to look at me as a real man. I needed to confirm my manhood again."

On a comical note, the event that initiated Nick's quest to find someone was an episode of *The Oprah Winfrey Show* in 2006 (he claims he just happened to be watching it that day). The topic of that show was "Sexless Marriages," and it opened his eyes to a fact which shouldn't have been as startling to him as it was. He was not alone. The realization of the fact, that there were indeed thousands if not millions like him, set him on a journey that at the beginning failed to prove rewarding.

"My mind became a sponge for the next two years," said Nick. "I began scouring the web looking for those people out there just like me. I wasted a lot of time on a variety of websites that promoted memberships for people wanting an affair. I met a lot of whacked out people on those sites like women who enjoyed being spanked or couples looking for a third wheel. I still wasn't exactly sure what it was I wanted in an affair, but I knew what I didn't want."

And then, enter stage left: Tammy. Nick met her on a blog site for people in sexless marriages. Tammy had read one of his blogs on a blog site there and they exchanged emails. Tammy had made the critical mistake that so many women do, she settled for something less than she deserved in order to be married. Her husband was an engineer who made it obvious he felt he was better than her. Tammy said he talked to her as if she were a small child. As their marriage progressed, he began to reject her both sexually and emotionally. She couldn't take it anymore. She too was looking.

It is at this point in the tale that I will bow out and let Nick take over the narration.

"In the beginning of our affair she just wanted sex and nothing more. We are not an obvious couple. She was twenty-nine and I was forty-six, so seventeen years separates us. She is far more sexually experienced than I am. She claims I'm number twenty on her list of sexual partners.

"Within a week of meeting we were holed-up in an airport hotel together. I remember the fear I felt as if I was crossing some forbidden boundary that would brand me forever as a cheater. I remember thinking I would spontaneously combust for these sins. Whatever fear I experienced was easily overcome by my need for contact with another human being. We made love for hours that day. I didn't think something like that would ever be possible for me. She was amazing. She had orgasm after orgasm, and with me. It quickly shattered all of those negative memories implanted in me by my frigid, asexual wife. I was capable of providing pleasure to a woman. I was good at sex! I watched her closely as we made love, amazed she could just let go of any inhibitions she had and be in the moment. Our first experience was more than I ever hoped it could be.

"Once we realized we had found something we both desperately needed, neither of us were willing to let it go. We established a single encompassing rule for our affair. It was simple - no feelings or love allowed. Neither of us wanted to drastically change our lives. With our rule in place we began our 'thing' as we called it.

"We would meet after she got off work. She would book a room at our favorite hotel weekly. We even have had rendezvous in each other's homes when the spouses were at work and the kids were at school and we needed a quickie. She began going on business trips with me. She would stay at the hotel playing in the pool while I would be out for the day. We would share dinner, conversations and, of course, make fabulous love to each other all night long. We were developing a great relationship, both in and out of the bedroom.

"We both made it a point early on to address each other's sexual fantasies. We were in Dallas a few weeks ago at this great hotel overlooking the city. I bent her over in front of our window in our hotel room. There was a traffic jam on the freeway just outside. Cars were just a few hundred feet away from us, I pulled her hair lifting her head so she could see the cars. I told her they were watching me fuck her hard, that they knew what she was doing. She went crazy, cumming three times in ten minutes and then collapsing to the floor. We have had many experiences like that.

"One special night, on an out of town trip, we were enjoying drinks and conversation at a restaurant and I felt my first twinge of feeling of love. The thing I had so strongly forbidden was in my mind. It was just something I couldn't explain but it was real. Later that night as we made love it was euphoric, I can't explain it but it was different and powerful! Our rule that we had so carefully crafted quickly disappeared and the first 'I love you' was uttered by me. I feared saying it, but it had to come out. She kissed me deeply and said she loved me too. She too was scared to say it, knowing it was against our rules.

"Our sex is better today than it was at the beginning. Our passion for each other has grown over time. Our affair has lasted just over two years. We still see each other several times a week. We still travel together when we can. We now have no issues with saying 'I love you' almost every time we are together. We are currently in the process of leaving our spouses so that we can be with each other every day for the rest of our lives, uninhibited.

"I can't tell you what she really sees in me. I was somewhat wealthy at one point but that was before the 2008 recession. My money was gone long before I met her, and I am anything but rich today. We just have an amazing connection. I may tell her about this to see if she wants to tell you why, but I have no doubt that she loves me unequivocally.

"I am realistic about our future. I know there are no guarantees in life. It's for that reason that we live in the now. I have found happiness for the first time in a very, very long time. I would not recommend an affair to anyone. It's difficult, lying is not fun. Guilt is real and so are the risks. If I had this to do over again I would have just ended my marriage and moved on. But, I would not trade this experience for anything.

I Do, Uh, Not Really

"Here's to the husbands who've won you, the losers who've lost you, and the lucky bastards who've yet to meet you."

- Dermot Mulroney as Nik Mercer in The Wedding Date

Fall is such a lovely time of year for a wedding. The colorful fall foliage creates a breathtaking backdrop for the glowing bride in her white gown standing proudly beside the handsome groom. Our story begins with such a wedding, a wedding involving a stunning twenty-four year old bride named Megan who was blossoming in the prime of her youth. Escorted by her adoring father, she walked down the aisle on a gorgeous Saturday afternoon twenty years ago in October. . There was a royal element to it all as she entered in her grand dress, a long white train dragging behind her. It was a grandiose site to witness I'm sure. There were eighty people in attendance to witness the ceremony including three bridesmaids and a maid of honor. She chose to wear a hat rather than a veil that day which was a brave decision on her part. The veil would have been much safer, for the veil could have well hidden her covert secret from the gallery of witnesses who had gathered in silent but doting celebration. The secret was that there was one person in attendance that didn't want to be there. Unfortunately, that person was the bride, and she was putting on her best bridal poker face to conceal it.

We sometimes hear about a bride or groom who gets cold feet at the eleventh hour and can't go through with it all. As a final resort, a last-minute intervention group convenes to reassure the hesitant bride or groom and coax him or her back to the ceremony. Should this tactic fail, some unlucky person is assigned the unwanted task of informing the guests that there won't be a wedding after all. For every such incident of cold feet, I bet there is another one like Megan's in which the show goes on, even when the starring actor or actress doesn't want any part of it. It's easy to understand how it can happen: the invitations sent out, the venue reserved and stacks of invoices paid in advance for catering, photography, entertainment, etc. To a reluctant bride such as Megan, it all looks like an accumulating snowball barreling down the hill. Its swelling size and hastening momentum are intimidating, overwhelming any declination she may be considering.

You're only supposed to get one bite at the apple when you get married. If you're a young twenty-four year old bride, you've supposedly succeeded at finding the perfect guy who sweeps you off your feet during a romantic courtship that culminates with your fairy tale wedding. In the case of Megan, she was committing the ultimate marital sin - she was settling.

"I wasn't happy," states Megan. "Something was missing in my life. I could easily see that my wedding wasn't going to be the fairy tale I had hoped for. The signs of a subpar relationship with my future husband were ever present. To say that our sex life was dull would be an understatement. I kept telling myself there was potential for a fulfilling relationship with this man who was fifteen years older than me, but my self-soothing assertions were growing less compelling each day."

Besides a lack of intimacy between them, her doubts were being fed by a burgeoning career at a local casino. Her skillset and natural talents were ideally suited for this profession, a fact that was soon recognized by upper management. Within the first year she was promoted twice, the second time to a high profile middle management position with a level of responsibility rarely attained by someone so quickly. While the casino was proving to be a promising environment for her career, it was also serving as a tempting foray of questionable, selfish indulgences. Says Megan, "I was vulnerable, about to be married in just a few months, and in the eyes of many men, looked the best I had in a long time. All of this in an environment where affairs were abundant, morals were non-existent and sin was everywhere. It was a whole new world."

Temptation came knocking on Megan's door in the form of a tall, dark and very handsome man named Brett. There was an immediate attraction between the two of them, and the idea of a last fling before her fall wedding was dancing in Megan's head. She took advantage of each and every opportunity to be near him and hopefully catch his eye, and more, every day at work. And one day, she indeed got more from Brett. Brett let her know flat out that he was interested in more than flirtatious glances between them. He wanted and craved her in all the ways Megan had fantasized about. The ball was now in her court. There was a lot for a girl with a strong Catholic upbringing to consider.

"I was both euphoric and conflicted at the same time, said Megan. "I was ingrained with strong morals throughout my upbringing. I really do have a good heart, but I felt this void in my life. To fill that void I needed a man, a man who knew how to make me feel like a woman. A man who would treat me as a sexual creature, yet still love and appreciate the person I am. I wanted the whole package."

Happily for Megan, Brett proved to be a masterful chef when it came to intimate and romantic delicacies. Megan loved every dish he was serving, and an illustrious affair that didn't disappoint was now on the table.

"It evolved into a tumultuous, mind blowing affair that I controlled, and it felt amazing! As the ominous wedding day approached, I knew I was no longer a willing bride, but everything was in place and paid for, and it was too late to stop it all. I knew no one would understand. I had to go through with it. Yes, it was a mistake to walk down that aisle. I do realize that was a tragic error on my part."

The two of them worked together at the casino at night, and they spent their days at a local hotel thirty minutes away. Brett was the same age as her fiancé and married with two children. He would drop everything to see Megan if she could get away. He also knew how to completely satisfy the sexual desires of a woman, ravishing Megan in ways that she never knew existed. Brett had the expertise to quench Megan's sexual thirst and then some. She was instantly addicted and couldn't go a day without talking with him, not even during her honeymoon. "The only romantic conversations I had during my honeymoon were with Brett," she admitted. "What a shame. The resort we stayed at was nice. That's about all I can remember about those five days."

For Megan, her real honeymoon was with Brett, and it was an ongoing one that never seemed to cool down. "He literally made me feel like a goddess, and he fell in love with every inch of me, "said Megan. "No woman is ever completely confident with her body, but I came close to feeling that way with Brett. He made me feel sexier than I had ever envisioned myself to be. His desire for me was 'off the charts,' and I was the total beneficiary of that desire. We soon outgrew the local hotel habit. We took more and more chances, even traveling for long weekends together. I wanted to do it everywhere with him. We'd park the car in public places. We replayed the grocery store scene in the movie, *Sea of Love. It was so intense!* "

Megan and Brett continued seeing each other for almost

ten years. Megan eventually discovered that sexual prowess and romantic outings don't necessarily pave the way for eternal love. The dynamics of life intercede; in this case, Brett lost his job, an event that moved him outside of the one-time easy reach of their everyday life. Their time for rendezvous was much more limited from then on, and their dates took much more planning and coordination. What's more, Brett was unable to find work, forcing Megan to foot the bill for their excursions. Over time, the lying began to take its toll on Megan internally. "After a while you just get tired of all the cheating, lying and sneaking around," confessed Megan.

From time to time, they had discussed the option of leaving their spouses in a coordinated effort to pursue a life together, but it was more 'after sex pillow talk' than anything else. Megan eventually ascertained that Brett was never really going to leave his wife. After a while, Megan wasn't even certain he was what she wanted anymore, whether or not he would ever go through with it. As in many affairs, her relationship with Brett simply vanished into the abyss.

The adrenaline that had emanated from her affair with Brett made her hungry for someone else to replace Brett to give her that same kind of sexual experience. She tested the waters a couple more times, but by then, Megan was no longer a young, bedeviled 24-year-old bride. "I knew I was never going to be happy with my husband, and he didn't deserve the woman he called his wife. I thought if I was going to continue to cheat on him, I wanted it to be over so I didn't have to feel any more guilt. The hardest part of an extramarital affair is learning how to forgive yourself. I left him the house, got an apartment and eventually left my job at the casino. I then went and got some much needed therapy."

Today, Megan is a free woman. She is free to find someone of her own, outside of the shadows of her past with Brett and the casino. As Megan and I wrap up our time together, she sums up our conversation with this closing statement:

"Those years with Brett were both the best and worst years of my life. The variables that make up an affair are never ending. As much as I ask God for forgiveness for my past mistakes, I also ask for direction and guidance, and the strength to keep going. I don't know what the future holds for me, but I am ready for it and I embrace whatever new adventures await for me."

I Wish My Mom had Continued Her Affair

It's funny that you're calling me tonight.
And, yes, I've dreamt of you too.
And does he know you're talking to me? Will it start a
fight?
No I don't think she has a clue.

Well, my girl's in the next room sometimes I wish she
was you
I guess we never really moved on. It's really good to
hear your voice
Saying my name it sounds so sweet coming from the
lips of an Angel
Hearing those words it makes me weak and I never
wanna say goodbye
But girl you make it hard to be faithful with the lips of an
Angel

-   Hinder, Lips of an Angel

Everyone is different, and when I started interviewing people for this book, I knew I'd have opinions and stories from across the spectrum. One of the most fascinating confessions came from a woman named Brenda.

"Many people say that they would never cheat on their spouse, but in my mind, that is an idealistic and preposterous thought, which may sound surprising coming from a woman."

While I was expecting a story of a current, or prior, relationship, she instead focused primarily on the philosophical questions of having an affair. Brenda's interview was nothing short of provocative. Her views certainly clash with traditional beliefs and though many will find her views uncomfortable, I'm sure many share her opinions. This is Brenda's story in her own words.

"I'm sure many of those same people have experienced a co-worker looking them in the eye for a second longer than they 'should.' Others have probably felt a sudden flutter when a friend intentionally brushes up against them. I'm sure many have felt a rekindled desire for an old flame after rediscovering them on Facebook, or on another online forum. I honestly believe that everyone gets lonely at some point in his or her marriage, and it's during one of these windows of time that we stray outside of our wedding vows, even if it's only in our fantasies.

"If you haven't experienced a moment like that before, then let me tell you how you feel when you garner the attention that you so desperately crave. It lights you up inside. It makes you feel alive, even if it's for the briefest of moments. It is in that instance that something inside of you turns on, something that has lain dormant for far too long and that you know is long gone at home. It's something that you didn't realize was missing, but that brief suggestive look in your co-worker's eye, or that brush against your shoulder, reminds you of what once was, and what could be again. It's at that moment that you can choose to act or choose to walk away. That is why we have free will.

"Yes, I have had an affair, and I can say that it was a truly wonderful experience-one that I cannot forget even if I wanted to. The man with whom I shared that relationship brought rapture into my life that I had never before experienced. Words such as passion, love, excitement, warmth, desire, not to mention mind-blowing sex, were not part of my daily vocabulary prior to meeting him. My time with him blew away any expectations I had envisioned prior to my affair with him. I wasn't planning on meeting someone like him, nor did I want to stop seeing him, as I finally did, but life is like that. Doors open and close continuously. I wish I could simply open that door again, renew that relationship with him and feel him against me.

"I've been thinking a lot about why I chose to have an affair and yet never considered the idea of leaving my husband. I know that many people think that people who 'cheat' on their spouse are selfish cowards. Their reasoning seems to be that if you don't love that one person anymore, you should make the choice to leave him or her before you start seeing other people. I can understand that line of reasoning, but those types of decisions involve many more players than just you and your spouse. For me, I'd lose so much if I left my husband. I'd hurt my family, and I know I'd never be able to find someone who is as crazy about my children as their Daddy is. Don't categorize me as selfish for choosing to keep my family intact while I get my emotional and sexual needs met elsewhere!

"I have firsthand experience witnessing the consequences of what happens when someone leaves his or her family in order to pursue someone else romantically. My mother left my father so she could marry his best friend. Their relationship started out as an affair, as my mother was not happy being married to my father. I get that. I am not 100% happy being married to my husband either. Are there couples out there that are 100% head-over-heels in love with one another? I want to believe so. If there are, I'd like to meet them. But I digress.

"My mother hurt my father by leaving him to satisfy her own selfish desires. It's something he never got over, even to the day he died. What's worse is that after he died, she told me she wished that she had tried harder to make things work with my father. She hurt me too by bringing me into an abusive household where I was always treated like a second-class citizen. As a result of her own personal quest to find love, she ended up hurting two people who loved her very much. However, if instead she had continued her affair with my dad's best friend, she might have learned that she could get her 'needs' met and avoid hurting my dad at the same time. Then, both my father and I could have escaped the pain she inflicted upon us. Perhaps, she was just afraid of getting caught, or maybe the way she was raised dictated that if you're not happily married, you should get divorced, even at the family's expense. Interestingly enough, I found out later that my grandfather had many affairs, and my grandmother knew about them, yet she stayed with him until the end. I can't help but think that if my mother had continued with the affair a while longer, she would have discovered what type of monster my future stepfather really was, and perhaps, she would have left her family intact.

"I have a problem with the word 'cheating'. Where does that word come from? From an early age, we have this concept that God wants us to be monogamous shoved down our throats. Society also foists this idea upon us because, obviously, a society made up of stable family units works better. But think of it this way: in nature, very few animals are monogamous. It doesn't seem natural to be monogamous. If indeed we are supposed to be with only one person until 'death do us part', then why do people feel compelled to look elsewhere for whatever they are not getting from their spouse? Don't you think that it would be genetically ingrained in us to be monogamous if it was indeed 'natural'?

"The obvious question for me is: 'How would I feel if I was to discover that my husband was having an affair?' That is a fair question. Would I be able to forgive him? Would I leave him and break up our family just like my mother did? Would I risk my children resenting me the way I resent my mother? I am guessing that I'd feel jealousy. What is it that 'she' does for him that I don't do? Is 'she' prettier? Does 'she' have a nicer body? Why does he feel like he needs to be with 'her'? Could I provide him what 'she' does?   I think I could suppress any vengeful response, or perhaps I am saying that because I am the one who has had the affair. Sometimes I wonder if what I really desire is an open marriage.

"At this point in my life, I can't say whether or not I will ever have an affair again. Right now, with a full-time job and two young children, I barely have time to breathe. I can say that what I had with the other man is something that I still think about to this day, and one day may pursue again."

I Know Not Where the Birds have Gone

A little voice inside my head said, "don't look back,
you can never look back."
I thought I knew what love was
What did I know?
Those days are gone forever
I should just let them go but -- I can see you --
Your brown skin shining in the sun
I see you walking real slow and you're smiling at
everyone
I can tell you my love for you will still be strong
After the boys of summer have gone

-   Don Henley, Boys of Summer

I got an email from a man named Gus one day. He told me that he heard I was looking for stories from people who had experienced an affair and wanted to know if I would be interested in hearing about a one-sided affair. I emailed him back that I didn't know what he meant by "a one-sided affair." Unfortunately, he told me, and I wish now that I had never known.

Gus served our country with pride in his years of military service. After leaving the military he made some very good financial and career decisions which would garner him a degree of financial security that many would envy. Gus has made many great decisions throughout his years and has accomplished much. However, few people are strong in all facets of their life, and unfortunately, his love life hasn't been nearly as fruitful.

Gus was married for 35 years. It was his wife's third marriage and she brought three kids into the matrimony as well. Gus took them in and helped raise them as if they were his own. Gus said it didn't take long to start realizing a high degree of dissatisfaction in his marriage. His wife always seemed to be complaining about something, and soon the criticisms began outnumbering the 'I love yous.' Towards the end of his military career, Gus served in Iraq during Desert Storm in 1990. Gus divulged to me that while other soldiers serving in Iraq received letters in perfumed envelopes full of romantic declarations of love, the letters he received were riddled with grumblings and grievances about his wife's life and how it was all his fault.

Things only got worse when he returned home. Her badgering became a part of the daily routine of life for him. While those around him recognized his achievements and successes, she only belittled him with disparaging remarks. There was little joy in Gus's life when he was home, which is why he readily accepted a promising opportunity in another city. It was a management position which would compensate him very well, a fact that his wife was very in favor of.

It would also provide him some unique challenges that would engulf a lot of his focus and attention, giving him an excuse to be away from his abhorrent domestic environment. He was looking forward to getting lost in his work.

Upon his arrival, Gus found something even greater to get lost in, a fellow employee named Lisa. When you're in a horrible marriage full of strife and verbal abuse, it's easy to hide it from your neighbors, colleagues and even family if you only see them during holidays now and then. You can't hide it from other people in similar marriages though. They easily see through the façade. When they meet you they can detect the lonesome spirit inside of you. They know what the lie looks like as they too are living it. Gus and Lisa recognized this about each other right from the start. In addition to being able to relate to her marital life, Gus found Lisa to be drop dead gorgeous. For him it was love at first sight.

Lisa's husband was very controlling and kept her at bay through an endless bombardment of verbal abuse. It's truly amazing how many gorgeous women there are out there who are completely insecure about themselves due to years of being put down by their husbands. Lisa, like many women in similar circumstances, appeared vivacious and effervescent on the outside, but inside she lacked confidence and self-esteem.

"I immediately felt a zeal to expose her to life much

more than she was accustomed," said Gus. "We started out with some very enjoyable and lengthy lunches. We both had a lot of freedom at work. Soon our lunches led to us traveling together on business trips, sometimes of a week-long duration. We went to Tampa Bay, the California Coast, Dallas and Saint Louis just to name a few. We both loved theater and sushi and we enjoyed experiencing those things together in each new city we traveled to. It was such a wonderful time and a true escape from our decrepit home lives."

Gus is a true gentleman and refused to disclose any of the intimate details of his affair with Lisa. He did tell me how strong he felt when she was in his arms. Her love for him gave him a sense of confidence that he had been lacking for decades, a confidence that gave him the strength to file for divorce from his wife one day. "I knew I had to leave at that point," interjected Gus, "as I only had a couple ounces of pride left in me by then."

Not surprisingly, his wife dragged out their divorce proceedings for as long as possible, milking the situation for as long as she legally could. Finally, three years into their affair, it was done. He was free, legally and morally, to love any woman in the world of his choosing. There was only one woman however that he had any interest in loving, and that was Lisa.

Like Gus, Lisa spoke constantly about leaving her spouse one day and running off together. She also expressed a lot of fears about leaving her husband. "My friends told me I was crazy to wait around for her," said Gus. "They told me that there are millions of women out there in bad or even abusive marriages who continually talk of leaving one day, but never do. I knew they were right. Most of the time it's probably due to a lack of resources to help them, financially or emotionally. I felt that with the combination of my devoted, unquestionable love for her and my financial resources that I could alleviate all of her fears and help drive her to the Promised Land where we could live happily ever after."

For the next five years, Gus and Lisa continued their love affair. Gus never pressured her to leave her husband, neither did he foist any expectations or time table upon her. He and Lisa would giddily talk about all the things they would do one day when they could finally be together.

She also conveyed her misgivings and trepidations of leaving her husband. She told Gus that she felt certain that her husband would take the house in a divorce. "Where will I live?" she would ask Gus. Remarkably, Gus bought her a condo in the part of town that Lisa had always dreamed of living. Lisa was overwhelmed by this gesture, but quickly asserted that her husband would get all of the furniture, and she didn't have the money to furnish her new lovely place. So Gus financed a whirlwind of furniture shopping, buying her a house worth of furniture fit for a princess, his princess. Whatever the concern, whatever the fear or obstacle was, Gus and his bazooka would blow through it, eliminating her anxieties one by one. Finally, eight years into their relationship, five years after Gus left his wife, Lisa agreed to see an attorney, for which, yes, Gus eagerly footed the bill.

Of course we all know how this story ends and if you, the reader, would like to turn the page to the next chapter, by all means go ahead. I wish I could.

A few weeks after seeing the attorney, Lisa told Gus that she couldn't go through with the divorce. After she told her husband about seeing an attorney, she said her husband immediately accepted a transfer to the west coast, a transfer that his boss had been offering him for some time. "He says a change of scenery will do us good," she told Gus. "He assures me things will be different this time. My family needs me Gus. I can't let them down."

Gus bowed his head with a heavy heart. It wasn't enough that he was losing his best friend and love of his life. Even worse, after all these years she was still willing to believe the lie or at least pretend to. He realized at that moment that his immense love matched with all the money in the world would never get Lisa past her insecurities and fears. She left him, promising to write once they were settled down and let him know where they would be residing.

Gus drove by her street the afternoon that she was set to move. He parked the car down the street and watched the moving truck as it pulled out of the driveway. Lisa was leaving him, leaving him with a condo full of furniture and a broken heart.

Gus said he never did get that letter and he never received a birthday or Christmas card from her. "That's what stings the most," admitted Gus. "I was so stupid, stupid for waiting patiently for eight years for something that I should have known was never going to happen. Deep inside, she probably knew in her gut she'd never leave. Our loving commitment to be together one day was as much a façade as her marriage. I need to stop now and get a martini."

I asked Gus a couple more questions but he stopped me. "You know the whole story," Gus told me. "I've omitted almost nothing except for the tears I shed for a long time."

Gus is seventy years old now. He's still single. One can understand his reluctance to get involved in another relationship considering his history. His social life is pretty much centered around the local senior center these days. "I don't know why I keep going back there, everyone is so old," he laughs.

He says he is OK now and at peace, although he still hates to open the mailbox during those periods surrounding his birthday or Christmas. I asked him if there's anything besides martinis that helps get him through those times he begins to think about her.

He then told me for many years he has secretly loved a sonnet by Edna St. Vincent Mallay. He particularly likes the lines:

I stand here like a lonely tree
I know not where the birds have gone nor why,
I only see the branches more empty than before.
I cannot say what loves have come and gone
I only know that summer once sang in me.

For Gus's sake, I hope that winter ends soon and that spring is around the corner.

Cynthia's Ride

Life ain't always beautiful, but it's a beautiful ride.

- Gary Allan, *Life Ain't Always Beautiful*

Most people don't just flip a switch one day and decide to have an affair. They come to that decision only after a lot of deep deliberation and reflection. It's not one big step, but a series of little steps. Like a little kid standing at the edge of the pool contemplating the idea of jumping in, they're timid, nervous, a little afraid, and yet they know they want to feel the water--and eventually they do. Of course, after experiencing the elation of that initial timorous jump, they immediately go about jumping, even leaping, into the pool for hours on end until exhaustion sets in.

Cynthia is a wonderful lady I had the pleasure of meeting one day. She is a sizzling brunette that attracts men's attention when she walks into a room. She loves football and is an avid fan, and is highly educated in the art of the game. She can easily hold her own in any conversation about the X's and 0's of the game with the guys at the local sports bar. Be warned, if one of her favorite teams is a rival of yours, you'd better bring your "A game" if you want to engage her on game day. If a ravishing brunette who loves football doesn't sound like the perfect woman for just about any guy out there, there's even more to her than that. She is a passionate woman who values family and honor. She works full time, yet finds the time to decorate the house for Christmas, making sure everything is perfect. So, why isn't her husband idolizing her? Why doesn't he make sure that she has every reason to stay at his side? Why isn't he constantly fueling her passion and ensuring that her presence is always appreciated, that her heart is always filled with love and that her body is desired exponentially? I don't know the answer except to say that some men are just plain stupid.

After learning the scant details of her experience in an extramarital relationship, I asked her to elaborate on it, sensing that her story was one to which many people can relate. Here are Cynthia's words:

"I've been married for over 30 years, which seems like forever. I never in a million years thought I was capable of having a relationship outside my marriage. It's not that my marriage is awful. It's just not great in the area where it matters the most to me in this stage of my life: passion. For years it was all about making a good home for my family. I raised my children and willingly sacrificed the small things in life to give them a happy environment. So, now my children are grown.

This should be the time my husband and I reconnect, but how do you get that passion back that has long since been gone? It's not that I don't love him. He's my husband and a wonderful father to my sons, but the awful truth is I don't have a desire to make love to him anymore.

"So I found myself one day surfing the web and came across a personal website that had ads listed by married people. I had no idea what I was doing, but I decided to create profiles just to see what might happen. Deep down I told myself I would never go through with meeting anyone. I just wanted to feel desired and wanted by someone again. I wanted a man to lust after me.

"I was blown away by the responses I received. It took several months before I finally considered meeting someone in person. It was only after countless emails, instant messages and phone calls that I felt comfortable in doing so. I had only been with two men before: my husband and another man before my marriage. To say I was nervous is an understatement. We planned to meet for a drink and go to a hotel afterwards. By the time I met him I knew I wanted him. The drink was preliminary. I would have gone straight to the hotel. We continued to see one another for about six months. It was a wild and crazy ride. Between our times together the anticipation would grow. We couldn't wait to be in each other's arms. It was the most exciting time of my life. I have no regrets. Unfortunately it did have to come to an end as he told me that his wife was beginning to grow suspicious, forcing him to discontinue our relationship.

I asked Cynthia what it was about her lover that attracted her to him, considering the huge response to her ad.

"I think it was his persistence. He wanted me so badly. He would constantly tell me what he wanted to do to me, and he got me so hot and bothered. When we met for lunch for the first time, he walked me back to my car and kissed me like I hadn't been kissed in years. I was blown away. We got in his car and made out like two teenagers. If we had not been in a public parking lot, I'm not sure what might have happened. When we finally made love for the first time, it was good, but it really didn't get great until I overcame my nervousness. By the third meeting, we became very comfortable with each other."

In my conversation with her, Cynthia made the most interesting comment: "I can accept my husband taking me for granted, but I can't accept my lover doing the same." When I pressed her on this, she explained to me that after several months of not hearing from her former lover, he contacted her one day, informing her that the coast was now clear again and he wanted to renew their relationship. Cynthia went on to explain:

"We have met several times. At first it was like we were never separated. It was very intense. Our last meeting was the Friday before Thanksgiving week.

The intensity was not there. I told him later that I felt like he was going through the motions, and the excitement between us was gone. I told him I thought he was taking me for granted and I didn't like it. He denied it and told me he loved being with me. That prompted my statement about my lover taking me for granted. I told him it might be a good idea to take a break. That was code for "I think we had something special for a while but it's over".

In conclusion, Cynthia said that she is ready to turn the page on a new chapter in her life. "I want that excitement again," she says with a girlish grin.

Although Cynthia found the comfort, passion and love that she desired in the arms of another man, she has no illusions of ever leaving her husband. "The question of leaving my husband is a non-issue," she says. "I have thought about what I would do if presented with such a dilemma. I can't and won't leave my husband under any circumstances. Not even if I'm happy beyond my wildest dreams with someone else. I just can't hurt my family for my own happiness."

This is part of the irony for many people in Cynthia's situation. She and many others just like her lead a double life: one composed of acts of unfaithfulness on one hand, and on the other hand an unwavering devotion to preserve the family unit and structure. This paradox centered on the preservation of the family legacy and name heralds back to the most ancient of times and was even considered customary for families of title for centuries.

I don't know if Cynthia has found her next oasis of passion in the arms of another man yet, but if you happen to overhear a lovely brunette playing Monday morning quarterback at your local sports bar, it might be Cynthia. If you are interested in meeting her, bring your A game.

The Bittersweet Serenity of Sandra

Players only love you when they're playing.

-     Fleetwood Mac, *Dreams*

Alan sat on his couch putting the final words on his poem for Sandra.

  We breathed,
we lay together our mouths an inch apart,
and breathed.
There was nothing said or to be said.
We breathed each other in,
and breathed each other out.
We breathed,
As one.

Alan is a true romantic. He is totally in love and infatuated with Sandra and their story could easily read like a romance novel. It would probably go something like this:

Alan sat back and reread his latest romantic prose for Sandra. He often wrote poetry about their experiences together. Writing about her helped him to feel her presence during those times that they weren't physically together. Alan began to get lost in his words when his thoughts were soon interrupted by the sound of his back door opening.

"Anyone home?"

Alan smiled. He was now in a perfect place, the universe was now in alignment. The love of his life had dropped by. He wasn't expecting her, seems her coming by unannounced was becoming a common occurrence. The unanticipated nature of her visits made them all the more special however. They had only known each other for five months, yet their relationship was already at a point to which she could simply stop by on a whim and visit him. It was just another confirmation that their bond was growing at an exponential rate.

"I'm back here," he called out. Alan rose swiftly from the couch to greet her, getting there just as she closed the door behind her.

"Hi Sweetheart," Sandra said in a sweet but sultry voice as she leaned forward to kiss Alan. "And hello Oscar." She bent down to pet Alan's cat who had tentatively come out to greet her as well.

"Why don't you take your coat off and stay a while," said Alan. He watched her remove her coat, eagerly awaiting to see what outfit she had worn underneath. "Let me take your coat."

"Hi Sandra." Sandra looked to see the smiling face of Alan's tween age daughter, Amanda.

"Hello cutie," and Sandra walked over and kissed her on the forehead too. "I wasn't sure if anyone would be home when I dropped by and here I get both of you."

"I'm on my way out the door," said Amanda. "Going to the mall with some friends. You two can have the whole place to yourselves."

Alan watched her mosey out the door. Even his daughter was comfortable with Sandra, and why wouldn't she he thought? Sandra was wonderful and Amanda could sense the happiness that Sandra brought into her dad's life. He turned to gaze at his true love. She was wearing a blouse that teasingly showed him enough of her tantalizing cleavage through a camisole underneath. He enjoyed the imagery of her, reminding him of how much he adored her body. His eyes then ran down her jeans that clung tightly to her. Sandra took such good care of herself and he was the beneficiary as he was enamored by every inch of her physicality. She was twelve years younger than he and he still didn't know what it was about him that kept her coming back.

He reflected back to the day he met her. She came out of the blue. He was prepping his friend's rental property with a fresh coat of paint to welcome the hopeful new tenants. It turns out, Sandra lived in the same neighborhood in a nearly identical house, probably because they were constructed by the same developer. By coincidence she had recently remodeled her home and. Alan invited her in to offer up some ideas. He followed her room to room as she rattled off endless possibilities for the house. Alan was impressed with her sense of vision and her ability to see potential where he only saw en empty room. Alan offered her a cold glass of lemonade from the refrigerator and they sat together on the front porch swing. They discovered they had a lot in common. They both had two daughters around the same age who were driving them both crazy at times with all the drama that is common for girls that age. They also learned that they were both non-conformists to some degree and they each gave the twenty minute short summary of their lives up to now. Later that day she friended him on Facebook and things took off from there.

"Let me hit the rest room," said Sandra and she headed down the hall to the bathroom. Alan watched her every step. She was a yoga practitioner and a runner with the most beautiful body he'd ever seen. He was such a lucky man he thought. Alan went to his own fridge and poured them both a glass of lemonade, partially to be a good host and partially to cool himself down.

"Where are you babe, get down here," he heard her say in a somewhat commanding voice. He rounded the corner and saw her there leaning against the wall. She had removed her blouse, wearing only her camisole that came far short of hiding a delectable pair of panties that he hadn't yet seen. She must have just bought those recently he thought.

"Get down here, I've only got a couple of hours," she teased. Alan rushed down the hallway, following her into the master bedroom. He closed the door behind him, his hand barely off the doorknob before she was in his arms, invading his personal space, kissing him deeply, her eagerness meeting his passion. They had kissed so many times, and like always for Alan, it was like kissing her for the first time. With one hand, Alan caressed the firm muscles of her lower back, pulling her in closer while the he gently stroked her neck with the fingertips of his other hand, something that he learned felt so good to her. She clenched her hands behind his shoulders, drawing him in closer. Alan soon led her to the bed, pulling back the quilt in one quick motion just prior to the two of them falling on the bed together upon which Alan pulled off her camisole in similar fashion. His lips soon parted hers, making their way to her breasts that he was already caressing with his left hand as she exhaled upon his touching them. My God she was sexy as hell he thought. I will never be able to get enough of this woman.

Alan's body was responding in rigid fashion to her, but for now it was all about her. As he feasted on her breasts, his hand went down and toughed the inside of her left thigh. The incredible firmness of her thighs was complimented by tenderness of her baby soft skin. She opened her thighs for him, inviting him in, and Alan took the invitation. Alan slid the panties Sandra had purchased just for him all the way down her captivating legs. Sandra then aided in undressing him and they went about entangling themselves for the next hour making love in its most passionate form. There were no rules or protocols to their love making. Nothing was off the table for the two of them. They were both led by their passion for one another and the immense elation and indulgence they fed to one another.

They laid there afterwards, him atop her, both awash in satisfied glows. Alan gazed at her face. He was flooded with joy at how beautiful she looked as she laid there beneath him. This is love, he thought. Yes, the sex is great, but finding beauty in innocent moments like we are enjoying right now, just laying here... there's a word for this and the word is love.

They laid there in total bliss, talking, laughing and flirting, which drew them into another round of intimacy and sexual playfulness. Immediately following another foray of climatic satisfaction, Sandra hopped out of bed and began getting dressed to pick up her daughter and take her to yoga where they would work out together.

Alan watched her leave his bedside, immersing himself in the afterglow of the loving experience they had just shared, trying to hold on to it for just a little longer before rising out of bed himself and dressing. Something about their lovemaking always touched a higher plane of reality for him. It was ecstatic. Together they had both found a higher level of sensuousness that never diminishes. He began playing back in his mind after their first time making love that the two of them were like magnets and that when he touched her, she could sense her touching her very soul.

Soon his daughters would return and he would cook supper for them. He didn't know when he would see Sandra again. They rarely ever set the next date. The only promise for a future meeting was her customary 'See you soon' that she always said as she walked out the house.

He knew he'd see her again. She always came back. Hopefully for love, but if nothing else, to get away from her husband for a while.

Well, maybe it isn't your typical romance novel. You see, Sandra is married. It is here that the romance novel ends, and Alan must take over telling the narration of his story.

"I'm not sad when she leaves, assures Alan as I listen to him speak of his unique relationship with Sandra. "I really can't afford to be...I mean... she could decide to try to make things work with her husband and leave me cold one day. I do my best to relish each and every moment we spend together and not make it hinge on where we might be with each other in the future. Even though she isn't physically here right now, I feel her presence. I love her. I believe she loves me too. I will never get enough of her."

"The fact is, times with her are the best times of my life," he states. I should be grateful to experience the love I feel for you even once in a lifetime. Few people get to experience something as beautiful as this.

 "I understand why she stays with him. For one thing, she and I have only known each other for five months. They also have two girls, a ten year old and a fourteen year old. She's a great mom and has no intention of disrupting their lives by leaving.

"I try not to think about her life outside of me. It's all I can do to separate her from her marriage and family life, because to tell you the truth, I'm not sure what to believe. She says that they don't have a sex life anymore. I realize that's not unlikely. I do get the impression that they are closer than she lets on. That doesn't bother me as much as it might. I just want her to be happy. She sure makes me happy, which is why I accept things the way they are.

"We get along so well. You have to have open communication for a relationship like this to work. I won't lose her because of some silly disagreement, faulty communication or argument. I will only lose her if she decides to go back to him exclusively and exclusively be his wife. That is my biggest fear. Sometimes it keeps me up at night if I think about it, which is why I try my best not to.

"But on the other hand, she is out with him on his birthday date tonight as we speak and she keeps blowing up my phone with text messages. Even celebrating his birthday out on the town, she can't stop thinking about me. That gives me hope. On the other hand, he is a good guy, she's lucky to have him. She was wild and chaotic as a young woman when they met. Hearing her elaborate on that time in her life, I know she would have self-destructed without him.

Alan knows quite a lot about her husband, not just because Sandra shares everything with Alan, but also because he has met her husband, and her husband knows of his relationship with Sandra.

Yes, you read that correctly.

"Two weeks into our relationship, she sent me a text that read, 'Shit hit the fan', said Alan.

"She actually came clean about me that night with him. That was the first moment I realized I was falling in love with her, that she couldn't hide me from him. Obviously I mean a lot to her. She argued for me throughout the night and got him to admit that she was happier for knowing me. She confessed that she needed some happiness in her life, and so he agreed. I can't tell you why he would agree to that, I guess he just wants to hang on to her as much as I do."

"He told Sandra he wanted to meet me and we set it up at a local Oktoberfest celebration. Ah hell, let's just use his real name, Peter. He and I separated from Sandra so we could feel each other out. As we talked, I had been pointing out the beautiful women scattered in the crowd. Then I directed him at Sandra and said, 'That's the prettiest one of them all.' Peter looked at me and responded, 'That's my wife.'

"I told him, somewhat directly, that at the end of the day, it's he that would be there for her long after I'd be gone. He nodded and said, 'I knew what I was getting into when I married her.' He later told me that she wasn't planning on getting rid of me anytime soon."

As I interview Alan, I find myself envying how he can

just separate himself from Sandra's domestic life and so readily accept the fact that he may never play a greater role than he does now. Not being able to resist, I asked Alan bluntly, "Can you be content with the role you have with Sandra." Alan didn't flinch.

"That's easy for me to answer, Yes, I'm content" he stated. My focus is on appreciating what we have now, not what might be. Just holding her hand is blissful. Actually, so blissful that I count it as some of the best times of my life and that's just holding hands. I'm happy to have that good feeling even once in my life. In other words, I'm not begging for more, I'm basking in what we have.

"To love someone is to be an asset to them not a drain. Needing is a drain. In love, I am obligated to find the best in myself so I have better gifts to share with her. Being in need is not the best a person can be. So we somehow have to let go. It's not really that hard. It's about being present and not living for the future or in the past. And it's liberating. Because I don't have a need for her, when we sit together just holding hands, we find bliss holding hands. I'm talking about not thinking about the future, not even fifteen minutes later. If I was thinking about the future what would I miss now? And that opens the moment to bliss.

"Don't get me wrong, I wouldn't mind finding someone who I could appreciate as much as my married girlfriend. She doesn't expect me to be faithful but gets jealous when I do meet someone. I do talk to other women now and then, even went on a date or two. She gets crazy jealous. Then she gets mad at herself because she doesn't believe she has any right to feel that way given her situation.

"I'm aware this all probably sounds crazy to you, but this state I'm describing is all in the mind too, just as need is. This degree of love shared among lovers is the path to a higher ecstasy, something a lot of people dream about having in their lives, but few do I bet.

Alan and I talked more about his adoration of Sandra and what she brings into his life. He kind of wrapped it all up nicely when he said, "She's not just a lover. She's my friend and confidant. She's the fresh flower who brought my inner lover back to life. She's the gift that makes the ultimate present. I don't want to possess her even while we fill each other. I don't want to take her away although we remain so close to each other constantly that we're virtually one already. I want her to love her husband and children and live a fulfilled and rewarding life. Meanwhile, I'll take every minute of her that she finds the time to share with.

And so I left Alan, leaving him to sit back and travel to that higher plane that only Sandra can take him to. I don't know where the higher plane is that he travels to, or what it's like being there exactly, but the smile that I saw immersed across his face tells me it must be a pretty special place. He emailed me a poem that day that he said he wrote just after we parted.

> Sulfurous sentiments
> sweetly seduce

soaked seductress.
Sexuality sails
steamy seas
stirring synchronicity.
Satisfaction swelters,
sultriness succeeds,
sweat soaks.
Serenity.

Serenity, though perhaps bittersweet, is a great word to end this story with.

Free at Last

Well, your faith was strong but you needed proof
You saw her bathing on the roof
Her beauty and the moonlight overthrew ya
And she tied you to the kitchen chair
She broke your throne and cut your hair
And from your lips she drew, "Hallelujah"
Hallelujah, Hallelujah
Hallelujah, Hallelujah

\-   K.D. Lang, *Hallelujah*

This book has been a true labor of love for me. I wrote my interpretation of some of the stories in the book using notes I took during interviews with the respective men and women. Others submitted their own notes to me about their extramarital relationships, sometimes supplemented by love letters, and even pictures. Some people acted as narrators and wrote their own story, allowing me to edit and rewrite as I deemed necessary. And then, there was Stephanie. When it came to Stephanie's story, I simply sat back and enjoyed the mastery of a true storyteller reciting her yarn. In addition to being an avid writer and ardent storyteller, Stephanie possesses a comforting tone and a special quality about her that comes from the wisdom gained from years of life experience. Her presence calms the soul. I have even asked her to counsel a friend of mine who could benefit from her gift of understanding and maturity. I feel blessed that I was personally able to connect with her. She has made such a profound impact on me, I think the purpose of this book was for me to find people like Stephanie.

Stephanie met her husband, Frank when she was twenty years old. They were hippies back then, when their lives were all about "the love." Frankly, it always starts out that way, even if you aren't a hippie. If only we could hold onto that all-consuming love. But, unfortunately as time moves on, the raging flames of passion gradually die down without our even realizing it. The humdrum of life and all its complications wreaks its havoc. It was no different for Stephanie and Frank. After marriage, came the kids. He went to pharmacy school. At thirty years old, Stephanie severely hurt her neck in a job-related accident. She was a waitress back then, and her mishap left her thirty-three percent permanently disabled. She was unable to go to work. She gained a hundred pounds. She couldn't drive anymore. She felt certain that her life, as she knew it, was over.

Frank's pharmacy career proved to be a seductive temptress for him. He became addicted to some of the very drugs he was issuing to his customers. Stephanie said that by the time she finally left him he was taking thirty Vicodin pills a day on top of other non-prescribed pills. Eventually, down the road, he lost his pharmacist's license.

Whether it was the drugs, his character, or a combination of both, his life plummeted into an all too familiar downward spiral. I don't know all of the reasons why it happened because Stephanie didn't elaborate. However, after Stephanie's tragic accident, Frank began to resent Stephanie and the drastic changes to her body. He hated her extra weight and never stopped harping on her about it. As time wore on, his tongue grew more punitive. But, Stephanie suffered more than just the anguish of continued verbal abuse at her husband's hands. One night, her gall bladder began rupturing at two-thirty in the morning, and he refused to drive her to the emergency room because he said he 'had to work in the morning.' Somehow, she got herself to the hospital on her own. Upon recognizing her condition, the emergency staff immediately prepped her for surgery. Between the ramifications of the accident and the constant emotional battering from her pill-popping husband, Stephanie's life had become a living hell.

Yet, even the direst of circumstances in life still offer us a silver lining. After her harrowing brush with death, Stephanie found hers. Desperate to escape her painful reality, Stephanie decided to pursue a law degree. In order to gain access to law school, she first needed to earn her undergraduate degree. After consulting with her pre-law advisor, who encouraged her to choose a major she was passionate about, she chose to study music. She was already somewhat classically trained in both the piano and the clarinet.

While finding solace in her melodious studies during that particular time, Stephanie met another musician named Irene. Stephanie and Irene played together for four years in the symphonic band. They performed their junior recital together, a piano and baritone sax duet from the fifties. During those four years together, they listened to new music, discussed musical influences and styles, exchanged riffs and fed off of each other's ideas and energies. From all of this emerged a harmonious friendship that was even more beautiful than the musical harmonies they created together.

Now that you have read the background of this tale, I will bow out and let the real storyteller take over.

"I have breast cancer. I already had surgery. I start chemo Monday. I want you to drive down and be with me." Those were the dreadful words spoken by my dear friend, Irene.

"My heart sank. Irene was only thirty years old, vivacious and in the prime of her life. Irene is my super tall, blonde, butch lesbian friend from music school. She played baritone sax. I played piano. She had a tiny blonde mustache. She specialized in deflowering married women. She told me she was a vampire. She wore flannel shirts, drank too much, smoked too much and lived on a steady diet of diet Cokes and Doritos, but had a level of energy and verve that couldn't be matched. She was an irresistible friend.

"I on the other hand was a plain white flower, married with children and almost ten years her senior. Our lives were very different, yet we were like two peas in a pod.

"After our graduation, I moved over two hundred miles away to attend law school, which of course prevented us from spending much time together. As time went on, the windows of time that separated our visits grew longer. To add salt to my wound of missing Irene, my marriage was on the rocks, I was only half done with law school, I was overweight, over-stressed, very depressed and secretly suicidal.

"But none of that mattered: Irene was pointedly asking for my help. How could I not go to her? I drove down to meet her at the gorgeous house where she was house sitting for the weekend. The clear winter night was dark when I arrived. There were candles glowing everywhere on the deck, the sky luminescent with stars. Some of her friends were there when I arrived, but they slowly began to depart one by one until only the two of us remained. Irene poured me another glass of wine and suggested we take advantage of the hot tub. I shyly stripped off my clothes, trying to hide the Rubenesque proportions that Frank so openly loathed and slipped quickly into the water.

"Her fresh mastectomy scar was brutal, a stark contrast to her one remaining beautiful large breast. She told me the surgeon found full node involvement. Her back ached constantly. Later the doctors would discover she had bone cancer to boot. I didn't have any idea at that time, but Irene had already been diagnosed with stage four cancer. She was already dying, and I was completely in the dark about it.

"We sat side by side in the water for a long time, drinking wine, talking and behaving like a couple of giddy high school girls. Suddenly, she leaned over and kissed me ever so softly. It caught me by surprise. Her face looked fuzzy in the steamy night, her long blonde hair like a halo of light. I kissed her back, gently at first, and then with fire as my body suddenly craved her woman's touch. It was the first time a woman had touched me in that context and yet, that night it felt like the most natural thing in the world.

"When we finally made it to bed, she expertly and tenderly made passionate love to me. I tried to hide my body from her, but she relentlessly insisted I knock it off. In her eyes, I was nothing short of 'gorgeous'. She lovingly complimented me, telling me that my milky white flesh gave her the greatest pleasure and was the softest she'd ever touched. This was unbelievable to me because Frank failed to tell me how much he hated my body. She touched me everywhere. Her fingers and mouth created such intensity that I could not imagine living even a moment of life without her head between my legs. I was no longer a plain white flower. I was glowing pink, scented and wet.

"She gently refused my offer to reciprocate going

down on her that first night, saying her 'bush' was too intimidating to the uninitiated. Indeed, she had a veritable 'ZZ Top beard' compared to my own sparse bush. Hers was shocking in its wildness, a thing of very strange beauty.

"After that, my life was never the same. What began as one night of uninhibited, unconditional lovemaking evolved into a long distance, four-month affair in the midst of Irene's chemo treatments and my busy second year of law school. I drove down for her first eight treatments as family obligations and grades suddenly became unimportant to me. I sat with her as toxic chemicals dripped into her burning veins. I made tea for her when nothing else would stay down. Soon her beautiful hair started falling out in the shower, her ZZ Top bush suddenly gone too. I felt deeply ashamed for feeling glad.

"I loved her bed. An entanglement of green plants and twinkling lights surrounded it. A giant poster of KD Lang on a chopper on the ceiling above her bed watched over us. She always played music during our lovemaking. She was surprisingly not a fan of sex toys, but had magic fingers to make up for it. If she were feeling well enough, we would make love. On her bad days, we would cuddle and nap together, caressing and exchanging sweet kisses. We started going out to the local gay bar as a couple. Her lesbian friends were wary of me at first, presuming I was yet another one of Irene's married, and ultimately penis-seeking, lovers, but they soon realized I was not like those others and accepted me. Before long, they took me in as one of their own, opening up with me as if I were 'one of the sisters.' I was touched. I loved being out with Irene. For the first time in years, I felt safe.

"Irene came to my house several times too, which was harder, but it had reached the point where I couldn't bear to be apart from her. We slept together in the same guest room bed in the home Frank and I shared. Somehow he was either deliberately choosing to ignore our love affair, or he was just totally clueless. The idea that anyone, much less another female, would be attracted to me was likely so preposterous to him that it simply wouldn't occur to him that Irene and I were lovers. My children remained indifferent as only teenagers can.

"Unfortunately, even during the most turbulent years of our marriage, Frank still required intercourse from me. Sometimes, when Irene was with me, he would knock on the door, while our naked bodies were wrapped around each other under the covers. He would demand that I leave Irene to come 'talk to him.' I obeyed. When I returned to her, dirty with his seed, Irene would pout and refuse to touch me until I showered off his filthy scent.

"And then, I lost myself in the ecstasy that no one except Irene could make me feel.

"Loving Irene was everything to me that my marriage

was not. I loved the way her scent would stick to my face and fingers. I loved the way she helped me carry in groceries and take out the trash. I relished in her comforting physical presence and appreciated her musical genius beyond measure. I loved everything about 'us.' I felt like a dying plant that was suddenly watered. Nourished and thriving, I finally felt as if I were a part of a true, loving relationship.

"Finally, I offered to get an apartment for us near the law school so we could live together. I wanted to stop driving a few hundred miles a week to be with her. I wanted her to stop smoking. I began dictating to her to change her diet and implored her to start substituting fresh juices and fruits for her diet Cokes and Doritos. I felt compelled to intervene to heal her body.

"Ultimately, she stood her ground. She proved as stubborn and careless about her health as any man would. She did not budge. She did not want to change. As a result, we started quarreling. Frank complained about how Irene and I fought like lovers on the phone and about our astronomically expensive long distance phone bills. Back then, cell phone time was very expensive. I was intensely emotional. And Irene was in no position to make commitments; she knew she was living on 'borrowed time.' On some level, I think her defiance stemmed from her own fervent need to have her life back as she had known it.

"I ultimately sent her a rather cruel letter that ended our relationship. In retaliation, she immediately quit chemo, boldly determined to live and die on her own terms. In a twisted irony, her house flooded the next winter, decimating our one-time love nest. Concurrently, her pictures mysteriously disappeared from my closet. I'm sure my husband was to blame for that.

"Defeated, I slunk back to my miserable marriage, finished law school and Frank and I moved back down south.

"But not before I ran into Irene one last time, ironically, in a natural food store, in early spring. We talked for two hours in the parking lot. Standing there catching up like two ordinary old friends, it was surreal, as if no time had passed. She told me the full story of the flood. She was in constant pain by then, as the bone cancer had made its home inside her spinal cord. I felt genuine, unadulterated pleasure seeing her again. We exchanged phone numbers before we parted, but neither of us ever called.

"A few months later, I finally walked away from my twenty-one year succubus of a marriage. Irene would have been so proud of me.

"Later that same day, I received the call informing me that Irene had passed away. She was only 32 years old.

"Clinching the sad irony of it all, Irene died on the fourth of July, on Independence Day of all days. On this symbolic day of all days, I was finally free of my unbearable marriage, and Irene, finally free of the excruciating pain of her slow, untimely death. Free at last, my beautiful girl! I could almost hear her shouting it from a heavenly mountaintop somewhere above us: Free at last, my love! You are free at last!

"I often think this blonde vampire saved my life, that she literally shared the last of her lifeblood with me. Her love and acceptance began my healing process. She taught me that a woman's body is an amazing source of sexual and sensory pleasure. She cast out the dark insults spewed by Frank. She showed me that I was sexy, beautiful and delicious, just the way I was.

Living Out of a Suitcase

"Make no mistake, your relationships are the heaviest components in your life. All those negotiations and arguments and secrets, the compromises. The slower we move the faster we die. Make no mistake, moving is living. Some animals were meant to carry each other to live symbiotically over a lifetime. Star-crossed lovers, monogamous swans. We are not swans. We are sharks."

- George Clooney as Ryan Bingham in *Up in the Air*

I have always believed that everyone needs to get away from his or her spouse occasionally for a weekend. It gives people the opportunity to be their own person for a couple of days outside of the confines of work, and, in many cases, makes you miss the company of the person you love most. It's a healthy thing to get away now and then, in my opinion.

Chances are you might be craving a weekend to yourself, but imagine for a moment that your spouse leaves you every single weekend. This is the interesting predicament of one of my good friends who has experienced this for more than a decade. His name is Jacob, and he is one of the nicest individuals you will ever meet. He's one of those people that have a hard time saying "No" to people, and it can be easy to take advantage of his generosity and courtesy. He has sandy blonde hair and a giant serving of southern charm. He has that look and virtuous persona on the surface that moms like to see when their daughter brings a guy home. Like the other people in this book, his life is an intricate web that can be exhausting, yet there is an innocence about him that makes one wonder how he found himself in such a situation. His story is unusual and one that will make even the most verbal critic of extramarital relationships take pause. I will let him tell his story.

"It was a three-hour commute which seemed like eternity to me. I was tending to the normal Friday-morning activity to have the suitcases packed and ready to leave as soon as we arrived home from work. I could not convince my wife that this was not a good thing for us to be doing and that it was leading to my unhappiness. No matter what the circumstances were, we ended up leaving our home every weekend to reside at the in-laws from late Friday until late Sunday.

"We would make the three-hour trip back just in time to get to bed and get a few hours rest before getting up for work Monday at 5 a.m. I kept up the routine because nothing I could say or do could deter her from making the trip. I was ignored all weekend while she spent the time living as if she had never been married. She was living under her mother's influence as if she was a child and could not make any decisions for herself.

"I felt as though she would never commit to me, our marriage or our home. She was busy with her career as an elementary school teacher and seemed to have no interest other than 'her' family, by which I mean her mother and her former premarital life. I confronted her and threatened to not make the trip on numerous occasions. It became a weekly argument, one that I had grown so weary of. I would go only because I knew my life would be even more hellish during the week if I didn't. I considered leaving numerous times, but I kept hoping things would change and that she would want to be at our home and have a better life together.

"At first I tried to make the best of it. I am a good handyman and enjoy woodworking as a hobby. I took on the project of redoing my mother-in-law's bathroom, installing all new fixtures and tile. After that, I finished out her basement. That project occupied my attention for many weekends, but once completed, I had to face the fact that I would eventually rebuild the entire house since I would be sentenced to visit there every weekend for the rest of my life.

"We tried counseling, but to no avail. During one of my private sessions with the counselor, I asked him what he thought of the idea of us quitting our jobs and moving to her hometown to be close to her mother, so we could organize our lives geographically around her mom. I was surprised when he told me that although it would save me the frustration of the long commute, it wouldn't change anything. He said that she would still go to her mom's house every weekend--maybe even every weeknight--and that I would still be just as alone--even more so as I would be away from friends.

"I began talking to friends to figure out if I was crazy, or to at least get some advice. I just grew tired of not having a life, and having come from a very religious family that did not believe in divorce, I felt like I was stuck and doomed to be miserable. I finally just started staying home and living my own life every other weekend rather than endure the never-ending pilgrimage. My wife was furious at first, but finally relented and drove down by herself.

"As time wore on I grew more frustrated. I spent a lot of time on the web, at my mother-in-law's, as well as at home those Saturday nights alone. While surfing one night, an ad popped up for Yahoo Personals. For some reason, I didn't hit the red X in the upper corner as I customarily did, and I curiously decided to take a look to pass the time. Within a few minutes, I had created my own profile, complete with a blue-eyed avatar, and logged on to see what it was all about.

"I looked at profile after profile of both single and married-but-looking women. By about 9 p.m., I was getting tired, but one profile I clicked on caught my attention. Her profile displayed a picture with a lovely smile and flowing dark hair with beautiful highlights of lighter tones. There was a simple caption under her picture and a short profile. I had no idea that the profile page of this attractive woman would lead to a relationship which has fulfilled every need for attention, affection and friendship imaginable to me.

"I nervously sent her a message from my account, not quite believing what I was doing. Within a minute, I received a reply, and we began exchanging hellos. We went about telling one another about ourselves and about what we were looking for. She was a lonely, recently divorced mom with two children. I explained that I was married, which I was sure would be the point at which she would stop chatting. She just kept right on explaining her need to be happy and have friendships, and I echoed her sentiment. We kept chatting for over an hour and ended that night's conversation with, "It was nice chatting." I thought, "Well that was fun, but I will never hear from her again." I was wrong. The very next day I couldn't get to my computer fast enough. I signed in to messenger and, to my surprise, she was online. She buzzed me before I could say 'hi' to her. We chatted and it was as if we had known one another for years.

"We kept chatting and, over the course of the week, decided we should meet. I was extremely apprehensive as we were toying with the decision when and where to meet. We chose a public place that was about halfway between us, as we lived an hour apart. I almost backed out, feeling nervous and not really knowing what to do.   Believe me; I did everything imaginable to talk myself out of meeting her. As I was about to call her to let her know I wasn't ready for this step, my cell phone rang, and I heard her sweet voice.   It was all the motivation I needed.

"We met at our public spot.   We talked and decided it was safe to go to dinner.   She talked about her children and her divorce, and I explained my situation to her.   I was upfront and let her know I had no intentions of divorcing my wife, and to my surprise, she was fine with that.   I just laid it all out and told her that I was in need of attention, love, affection and simple company and conversation, all things I was not getting at home anymore. To my shock she simply replied, "I am good with that."

"Well, we have been seeing each other for five years now. I have completely stopped accompanying my wife on her weekend treks. Instead, I've spent every weekend possible seeing the woman who turned out to be the love of my life. I have never made any promises to her, and she is okay with what we have. We are more public than ever about our relationship. We take vacations when I can find an excuse to tell my wife, and have flown out to Vegas and Disney World.

"I am not telling this story to say I am proud, but rather to say, I had to fill a void. Right or wrong, I played the hand I was dealt. I don't regret my decision, and I look forward to the future. As I see it now, the best is yet to come."

Author's Note"

Two weeks after sharing his story with me, Jacob called me up and informed me that he was filing for divorce and planning on furthering his relationship with his beloved woman, whom he hopes to marry at some point down the road.

65,000 Text Messages of Love

But he's worth it
He deserves it
He may not be perfect
He's all the man I need

-    Whitney Houston, *Love That Man*

This is the story of Tara.

She loves that man.

I could be a lazy writer and simply leave it at that without shortchanging her story at all, for the saga of Tara and Danny can be summarized in just those four words. Any narrative or colorful vocabulary I may add here to the written canvas of this story will simply be repetitive in nature. There is no doubt that she loves that man.

For those who may question her love, she has 65,000 text messages between the two of them that she has saved and that's not even all of them. Every lonely man in this world should hope for a woman as dedicated as Tara. Her love for Danny is undeniable and irrefutable.

If 65,000 saved text messages can't convince you, then her patience and steadfast commitment will. Tara left a man otherwise known as her husband over five years ago after spending six weeks with Danny. Those six weeks convinced her that there was a better life beyond her broken marriage, that there were greener pastures past the constant years of letdowns and broken promises. That short time with Danny showed her what was possible when a woman does indeed meet the right man.

It only took six weeks for Tara to make the leap to a better life and abandon her former one, an existence dominated and plagued by a problem marriage. She was in a bad marriage for 23 years with a man named Jim. They had three kids together, the youngest one afflicted with a rare genetic abnormality called Sotos Syndrome. Daycare was financially unobtainable for them so Tara became a stay-at-home mom. Cracks began forming within the marriage when Jim was fired from a 17 year position. He rotated through a variety of jobs after that. Mostly the two of them and their kids, now in elementary school, lived on unemployment insurance, barely allowing them to survive check to check.

Jim undertook a new initiative to work on his own and start a business. Tara was thrilled that he would be establishing a family business that could create opportunity and wealth for the family. Because he would be working from the house at first, she started working to support his new endeavors.

"I was excited that he was willing to work on his own and saw good things coming from it," said Tara. "It didn't take long for that bubble to burst. I would come home most days to find that Jim had been sitting at the computer all day smoking weed. His perpetual state of being stoned explained why everything was alright in his world, while I was struggling to pay our bills. I would ask what he had done while I was at work and he would say, 'I cleaned the kitchen and vacuumed the rug.' I of course was hoping to hear something about paid work."

This sad play went on for many months. Soon, Tara was forced to begin resorting to the local food bank to feed her family. Tara begged Jim to help them out financially but he saw nothing wrong with how things were. He later did obtain a part-time job working three days a week, three hours a day. He would thrust his paycheck at Tara at the end of every month as if he had fulfilled his obligation to her.

"My resentment of him was growing at a fast pace,' said Tara, "but I needed to provide for the family, so did what I had to do to get by."

"It wasn't just the money, it was our lack of intimacy as well. I was so starved for physical affection. I remember sitting at the kitchen table once when he came in to get another beer and as he walked past me I began screaming inside my head, 'Why can't you touch me. I'm sitting right here, just come and put your hand on my shoulder?' Anything would have been welcomed. I just needed to be touched. It was one of the last simple pleasures that I could afford, yet remained elusive."

And then one day Tara read the subject line, "Why does life have to be so hard sometimes?" It was a subject headline for a personal ad that caught Tara's eye as she began searching online for someone who could provide the emotional support and physical contact she so craved. The ad was posted by a guy named Danny.

Tara responded to his ad, which resulted in a flurry of emails, followed by a first phone call which then led to a first date, which culminated with a first kiss that sent an electric shock down Tara's legs.

"Two weeks later we went for a picnic in the park," Tara explained. "We found the most isolated area of the park available to us. It was a lovely day and it seemed everyone was coming to the park to enjoy it. After a brief window of flirtatious behavior on both our parts, we quickly scooped up the blanket and the unopened picnic basket and headed someplace more private. We ended up on the futon in his basement. The wife and kid were gone and I still remember him stripping off my tight jeans and mumbling how gorgeous I was. No man had ever showered me with such flattery and praise concerning my body or how I looked. It's a quality about him that remains constant to this today. He made love to me that day in a manner I had never experienced with the perfect combination of both ravenous desire and gratifying tenderness. He made me feel like a total woman that afternoon."

Six weeks later, Tara broke up with her husband. When she told him that she wanted to split up, Jim shook his head in disbelief. Eventually the two of them would agree to terms: Tara would keep the house after living with her sister for a spell.

Unfortunately there is one small problematic detail that I have left neglected throughout this story that prevents it from being classified as a fairytale. Danny you see was married when Tara first met him, and sadly, still is to this day. He lives with his own sad tale of domestic misery, trying to raise a seven year old boy in the same house as his alcoholic wife. For five and a half years Tara has remained a single woman who has molded a relationship with a man she can't completely call her own. She even takes part in a blog titled, "I am the other woman" in which women who find themselves in relationships with married men gather online for support and advice.

"Yes, he is married," asserts Tara, "but ours is a bond that will never be broken. I will love him till the end of time. He's my heart and soul and we are so connected. I feel him with me always, even when he isn't physically with me. He's my last thought at night and first thought in the morning and consumes my thoughts during the hours in between."

Tara has a lot to say about her love for Danny, but she also has strong opinions concerning the other-woman syndrome. "Some people who blame the other woman have rocky marriages themselves and are afraid it may happen to them," states Tara. "Instead of addressing the issues with their spouse, they stick their heads in the sand and ignore things until it's too late. The other woman becomes the scapegoat and the issues in the marriage still go unresolved because that is easier than looking in the mirror. People don't accept that cheating is often a symptom of an already broken marriage and blaming the other woman is easier than looking at issues that caused the cheating in the first place. It is not possible to come in and break something that is not already broken on some level. No one knows what goes on behind the closed doors of a marriage. They don't know what is happening between the two people involved. Many couples put on a happy face to the outside world, when things are falling apart on the inside."

"Danny's situation was far different from mine," she explains. "Yes, he hasn't left, but it isn't because of his wife. He is doing what he feels is right for his son, Brian. Unlike myself, he needs to think for two. We live in a rather isolated area and his son is an only child. His drunk wife certainly can't be trusted to care for his boy. Danny has dedicated himself to being the stable parent, as well as confidant and playmate for Brian. To tell you the truth I wouldn't want a man who would walk away and leave his child with a woman who can't be trusted. As a mom I would never allow it.

"Danny juggles constantly between his business, childcare, maintaining his place fending off his wife and loving me. He's a mechanic and runs an auto repair shop on his property. It was always a dream of his and I would never ask him to give up his dream for me. I have supported this from the day he shared his dream with me. He is good and fair and just. He hates how people are taken advantage of when their vehicles need repair. He follows his heart when dealing with people and it's one of the things I love most about him.

The relationship that Tara and Danny have made for themselves is anything but simple. In some ways their story is of an enduring tale of love between two people who have overcome their muddled circumstances to share their lives together in a manner that works for them. In this perspective, their love is both enviable and admirable. However, one cannot help but feel that Tara is trapped in an "other woman" stereotyped relationship with a man, who despite repeated assertions, may never leave his wife and make Tara the exclusive centerpiece of his life.

Tara is used to being judged for her choices. Over the

years she has grown tired of explaining her actions and choices to various friends and colleagues and has eliminated those connections from her life for that reason.

"I remember when I used to tell people and defend our relationship," said Tara. "They said the usual stuff you typically hear - that he will never leave, I would assure them that this is different, that he will one day. Now I really don't speak to any of those people anymore. I don't want to hear the nagging questions and I'm tired of defending myself. I can't do it. It's almost embarrassing at this point."

Tara proudly states that thanks to their mutual commitment to making it work, they truly spend quite a bit of time together - on average about eleven hours a week. One can easily contend that there are plenty of married couples today who don't spend eleven quality hours with each other on a weekly basis. The amount of time that Tara gets to spend and enjoy with the man she loves beyond measure is indeed something that many women, both married and single, would covet. Yet, after getting to know Tara, I feel sadness within me because she deserves more.

But the quietude of my sadness is always interrupted by Tara's next declaration of love that Tara has for her man such as, "We are each other's sanctuary and you don't really know what that means...until you find it."

"Obviously he isn't here much of the time, but I handle it. When Jim was working, he was out of town a lot, at one point it was every other week, for a week at a time" explains Tara, "so I am used to not always being with the person I am with. That helps me a lot. When Danny is not here it is like he is simply away working. It also helps that I have 24/7 access to him through texting. He is always just a text away.

"Whenever my car won't start or it's making a funny noise, he comes right away and takes care of it. Same with any home repairs I can't handle myself. We're always there for each other when we're needed. His father was in the hospital for a couple of weeks at one point. He would drop by every day after visiting his dad and we would just hug and I would comfort him.

"Some days are rougher than others. Holidays are the worst naturally but I do always hear from him. I have heard from him every single day since the day we found each other. No exceptions, every single day. I think that's amazing. And the holidays, well, they are just one day. I have so many other days to be thankful for that one day passes by and we are back to us again.

"Danny told me that he felt that once Brian turned 12 he would be at a good age for him to understand the changes Danny wants to make in his life. Unfortunately that hasn't happened. At the beginning of the year Danny and his wife had a huge blow up. She was in one of her drunken stupors and he had come to see me to escape her. She was blowing up his phone with texts and calls but he refused to answer. When he finally returned home she was enraged. She got in her car to leave and crashed into a tree in the front yard. He said then that he was done with her, of course that was ten months ago and nothing has changed. He has asked me in the past to please not give up on him. I told him I hadn't and had no intention of giving up.

"He gave me a ring and I wear it all the time on my ring

finger. It's hard when someone sees it and asks if I'm married because I have to say no, but in my head, I'm screaming yes. We're married in my heart. God I'd love to say 'Yes I am married."

Tara can talk endlessly about Danny, the man he is and the incredible love they share. She can tell you countless little stories of their day-to-day occurrences. However, it's what she doesn't mention that concerns me. Never in five and a half years has there been a long romantic weekend in the mountains. There hasn't been a trip to the beach in which she tantalizes him in that new two piece bathing suit as they enjoy the combination of surf, sun, oysters and frozen margaritas by day and comparing their new tan lines by night. There's no mention of that celebratory evening out on the town in which she puts on that little black dress, the one that hangs in the back of the closet, that dress that's only worn for those special occasions. No mention of those rare nights when they go to the restaurant with the twenty dollar entrees, then dance the night away at their favorite night spot, concluding the night back in their bedroom where he unzips that black dress and she lets it simply fall to the floor.

Yes, it's those stories that I don't hear her talk about that prompt me to ask her the inevitable question, one that I hate to ask. "Will you do this forever?"

"I will do this until it no longer feeds my soul. If there comes a point where we stop growing and evolving, individually, or as a couple, then I will reevaluate our relationship and my part in it. Maybe then it will be time to move on.

"Today though that is not the case and I am willing to continue. I live in the here and now, and in this moment.

I have no reason to leave. He fills me with joy and love. I do not want to live with 'what ifs' so this must play out to whatever outcome the universe has planned for me and for us.

"We know each other so well. I have never been with anyone who just 'gets me'. He has never been loved just for who he is, so for him, that's really something that stands out to him. I give him something that no one else can, which is why I know he will always come back to me. I know he wants more, I have no doubt."

Tara pauses for a moment, pondering on a thought and then continues. "Brian would be the only reason I could accept losing him and be okay with it. Outside of that, I've been patient enough. And I know he wants more, I have no doubt.

"I used to have serious doubts now and then," she continues. "One day I realized that the only 'doubts' I had come as a result of other people's doubts and misgivings. I realized I didn't have any of my own and I started to listen to me. I know now that the only person I have to please is myself. The only person whose opinion matters is mine. It's my life, my heart, my choice.

"I love this man and he loves me just the same. It has nothing to do with where we live. It has to do with who we are when we are together. You can say that life gets crazy, but it's not unless you give it power to be.

"This is simply my life, it's just the way it is."

Just Like Bonnie and Clyde

<u>Bonnie Parker</u>: *What would you do if some miracle happened and we could walk out of here tomorrow morning and start all over again clean? No record and nobody after us, huh?*

<u>Clyde Barrow</u>: *Well, uh, I guess I'd do it all different. First off, I wouldn't live in the same state where we pull our jobs. We'd live in another state. We'd stay clean there and then when we'd take a bank, we'd go into the other state.*

- *Bonnie and Clyde*, 1967

The first part of Justin's blissful story of how he met Jessica and how her love transformed his life is a great story, but there is a lot more to it, as it turns out. Episode two is a story of love, heartbreak, espionage, secret agents and underground crime. It reads like the script of a Hollywood movie.

For many months after Jessica left, she and Justin exchanged emails, instant messages and Skype calls nearly every day. Justin later told me that he was going to Australia in September to spend ten days with her. While there, he was going to look for employment and had already set up a couple of networking meetings. His goal was to move to Australia by his birthday in December and live there permanently. He spoke of marrying her the following year. In preparation for doing so, he was already closing down his photography business and had turned down several high-paying gigs that would have conflicted with his timeline. After terminating his lease, he sold some of his equipment he used in his business, as well as some of his personal belongings that were too bulky to take with him. I thought he was crazy. I told him that this was a wave, a great movie, a hell of a wave. This would be a story he could tell at the senior center for years, as the old men would beg him to tell the story of Jessica, yet again. I told him to slow things down and think them through. He assured me he already had and was irritated by the fact that I wasn't supporting him in his quest to be happy.

And so time passed until it was two weeks before Justin's September excursion to Australia, and to say he was excited would be an understatement. His family and other friends voiced their reservations about this idea and his intentions of moving to Australia. It had strained his relationship with some of them. Justin didn't care: he was in love, and he was going to do everything he could to see her, and hopefully spend the rest of his life with her.

It was at that two-week juncture, at 11 p.m., after working a fourteen-hour day with two jobs, that everything came crashing down for Justin. As he walked up the stairs to his apartment he heard a commanding voice call out, "Are you Justin Baker?"

Justin turned around and looked down to the foot of the steps where the voice had originated from to see two well-dressed gentlemen. What came next was something he never saw coming. His life was about to self-destruct.

One of the men standing there looked like he could be playing linebacker in the NFL; the other was tall and lean but had arms and shoulders that were bulging in his shirt. Justin asked them what they wanted. One of them introduced himself as Mike Kreighton of the FBI and his associate as John Lemont of U.S. Customs. Needless to say, they had Justin's full attention and curiosity.

Mr. Kreighton asked Justin if he knew a Ms. Kimberly Billcott in Melbourne, Australia to which Justin shook his head, telling them they must have confused him with someone else. They asked him why he had sent packages to her house several times over the past six months. Justin informed them he had sent some packages to his girlfriend, Jessica Disgarnio, but that he had never had any dealings with a Kimberly Billcott. It was then that Mr. Kreighton told Justin, "I think we need to talk, Mr. Baker. May we come in?"

Over the kitchen table, the two gentlemen began the process of destroying the world that Justin thought he knew. They informed him that the lady he knew as

Jessica was indeed Kimberly Billcott from Melbourne. They then began to display copies of passports on the table showing how Kimberly went by several aliases. Justin was asked once again about the packages he had sent. He told the men about the romantic affair that he and Jessica had shared and that she had asked him to ship her some of her belongings that she was unable to take with her on her return flight. Justin proceeded to share some of the emails they had exchanged, as well as the pictures he had taken of her during their three months together. Even a macho stern FBI agent can recognize when a man is head over heels in love, so rather than interrogating Justin as they had originally intended, they began to recite the story of the real Jessica, a process that would take them until 2 a.m. the next morning.

As it turns out, Jessica was not an international music professor, but a smuggler. The niece and nephew she was raising back home in Australia were actually her children and her ex-husband was in jail serving a 25-year sentence for murder. She was one of the major players in a crime ring that smuggled knock-off items such as computers, music, movies, and luxury women's accessory goods into the country and distributed them as the real thing.

They told a story of how Australian authorities were cracking down on the illegal smuggling operations plaguing their country and that they were working in partnership with authorities in the U.S. and New Zealand. They went on to explain that the shipments

Justin had sent to Jessica had raised a red flag and that his recent purchase of an airline ticket to Australia had prompted their visit, as it was assumed that Justin was part of the operation. They finally ended the discussion with a warning that if Justin were to disclose any part of this conversation with her, he would be arrested as an accomplice. Mr. Kreighton handed Justin his card and informed him to call immediately if he heard from Jessica again.

Jessica called Justin the next day. He told her in the most normal-sounding voice he could muster that he was forced to cancel the trip due to a variety of reasons. He could tell that she wasn't buying it because she kept imploring him to tell her what was really going on. Justin stuck to his guns and told her he had to go. Jessica called him again but he never took the call. Mr. Kreighton came by the next day to ask what had transpired with Jessica's phone call. It was obvious to Justin that his phone was probably being tapped. For the next several weeks, Justin lived a paranoid life, wondering to what extent his phone and email were being monitored. He swore a couple of times that he saw black SUVs following him.

Jessica had brought love into his life, only to have it snatched away from him along with any sense of trust in what was real. Justin fell into depression. He sent out a Facebook status, informing his friends that he was going off the grid for a while and he would not be returning phone calls or text messages. He went into total mourning. At his lowest point, he took a road trip to the nearest beach. He arrived in the early evening, parked his car by the shore and walked down to the surf, cradling a newly purchased short barrel shotgun. There he stood in front of the water, eyes fixed upon the ocean horizon as if he were trying to peer into Australia in search of the girl who had completely deceived him. Who knows what went through his mind as his index finger rested up on the trigger, but he didn't contract his muscles. Instead, he let the gun simply fall into the sand where he left it as he sauntered back to his car.

Time heals all wounds, so they say. Months passed by and Justin began slowly getting over the big lie of Jessica and putting her behind him. In early December, Justin's birthday arrived. It was the day that he originally had planned to move permanently to Australia and celebrate with the woman he loved. Justin instead celebrated his birthday with a good bottle of scotch that night and got drunk for the first time in years. Sometime in the evening he passed out, only to be awakened by his cell phone. He answered it and heard a voice he thought he would never ever hear ever again:

"Happy Birthday, Justin I love you! I know you feel you know everything there is to know and I am so sorry -- I never meant to hurt you. I will see you sometime soon and we will talk and I will explain everything to you. I hope you are okay. I love you."

She hung up and Justin sat in silence, staring at his

cell phone screen, which displayed "unknown number". He debated what to do next, but the following day he did in fact call Mr. Kreighton to inform him that Jessica had called him, just to cover himself.

The story of Jessica would remain dormant in Justin's mind for several more months until early one Saturday morning, when he answered his front door to find Mr. Kreighton staring at him yet again.

"I haven't heard from her," said Justin in an irritated voice.

"I know you haven't, Mr. Baker. She's in jail. May I come in?"

Justin led him to the same kitchen table they had met at before. As soon as they were seated, Mr. Kreighton got to the point of the visit.

"Were you supposed to be in Charlotte, North Carolina, two weekends ago?" he asked.

"Yes," answered Justin. "I was supposed to manage a hockey tournament down there that weekend, but at the last minute I was assigned to a different city and my boss went to Charlotte instead."

"Did you receive a number of phone calls from the Charlotte area that weekend?"

"I don't know", answered Justin. "Ever since Jessica last called me, I don't answer my phone if I don't recognize the number."

"Well, the fact is you did," said Mr. Kreighton, and on that note he began to recount another amazing tale involving Jessica. Justin had posted his upcoming trip to Charlotte on his Facebook page and neglected to change it when he was diverted elsewhere at the last minute. Jessica in fact flew to Charlotte to meet Justin that weekend and approach him directly, face-to-face. She called his cell several times from the hotel where she stayed. The frequency of these calls triggered a red flag with the FBI, who dispatched a team of agents to the hotel. Upon arrival, the team started searching for her.

"You wouldn't have recognized her at the hotel, Mr. Baker," quipped Mr. Kreighton, "she had changed her look completely. She had become a redhead with a bob cut and had blue contacts. We wouldn't have recognized her either. The only reason we were able to nab her was the fact that one of our agents was walking past the elevators when the doors to one of them opened. Jessica stood at the back of the elevator, her exit blocked by a maid cart. She said, "Excuse me, ma'am. I need to get out. Could you move your cart?" She did so in a heavy Australian accent -- an accent that caught the attention of the agent walking by; he stopped in his tracks, boarded the elevator, and arrested her.

From the back of the FBI vehicle, Jessica asked that she be allowed to use her one phone call to call Justin. The agents informed her that since she wasn't an American citizen, she didn't have the right to a phone call.

"So instead she wrote you a letter," said Mr. Kreighton as he pulled an envelope out of his suit pocket. "I will need you to sign for the receipt of this."

Justin took it from him and looked down at the front of the envelope which read, "Please, please read this. I never meant to hurt you, Kim (your Jessica)". He gingerly flipped the envelope to read the following words on the backside, "I love you Justin! You will never know the love I had for you".

Six months have since passed. Justin still holds on to a high degree of resentment towards Jessica. Frankly, I think Jessica was faced with a dilemma that is one of the oldest in the book. When they met, she obviously couldn't disclose the truth to Justin, and once she fell in love with him, she was clearly scared of losing him if he knew the truth.

It was her love for Justin that ended up getting her caught and sent to prison. Jessica ended up being sentenced to 18 years in an Australian prison. Had she not traveled to Charlotte that fateful weekend, she would probably be free today. People will risk a lot for love and she clearly did that day.

Justin has yet to read the letter. He's promised me that we will read it together one day over a great bottle of wine. Being as invested in the story as I am, I can't wait for that day. Maybe that will be the first chapter in the next book.

If you enjoyed this book, please feel free to write and post a review at the online store you purchased it at. Reviews help a great deal in getting the word out about the book and I appreciate them a great deal. Thanks in advance.

Brad Rudisail

ABOUT THE AUTHOR

Brad Rudisail is a writer, musician and IT Consultant. Brad was a syndicated writer for eleven years writing a bi-monthly column for newspapers throughout the state of Georgia. He is a hired blogger and writes educational curriculum for online universities. He is an accomplished pianist and composer and has won regional and national awards for his musical work and has released six instrumental CD's throughout his career. He is also an IT consultant and serves a variety of clients across the globe as a network engineer and trainer.

You can read more about Brad and view more of his readings about the subject of this book at
www.theforbiddengameoflove.com

If you enjoyed this book, you may like his other book, Someday I'm Going To...

You can also email him at author.brad.rudisail@outlook.com